CHARMING THE ENEMY

IONA ROSE

AUTHOR'S NOTE

Hey there!

Thank you for choosing my book. I sure hope that you love it. I'd hate to part ways once you're done though. So how about we stay in touch?

My newsletter is a great way to discover more about me and my books. Where you'll find frequent exclusive giveaways, sneak previews of new releases and be first to see new cover reveals.

And as a HUGE thank you for joining, you'll receive a FREE book on me!

With love,

Iona

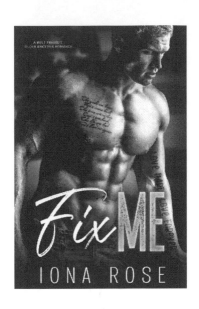

Get Your FREE Book Here:
https://dl.bookfunnel.com/v9yit8b3f7

STEPHEN

Early mornings in the office were my favorite time of the day. While most people dreaded reading and responding to their emails, I looked forward to it and did it first thing when I got to the office.

Most were from my team, other venture capitalists like me, but most were from entrepreneurs seeking funding. Those were the exciting ones. I loved sifting through the various applications to find gold. Fledging companies that required a bit of capital to fly.

A small company that sold jewelry had caught my attention. The owner, a woman called Marjorie had applied for funding and included a thorough business plan as well. Such people always got my attention. It showed they were serious about their future prospects.

My cell phone vibrated, and I picked it up without glancing at the screen. My attention was on Marjorie's email.

"Yes?"

A soft laugh came over the phone. A laugh that I'd recognize any time and which drew me away from my computer screen.

"You still haven't learned the polite way to answer the phone," Paige, my ex-wife said.

I laughed. "Have you ever known me to waste time on chit chat?"

I pictured my ex-wife seated on a lounger, getting as much of her skin tanned as possible or about to hit the shops for a shopping spree. She could be going for lunch at the club with her friends. That was Paige's life and she loved it that way.

"It's that attitude that ruined our marriage," she said, with no trace of bitterness in her voice.

I laughed it off as memories of the past swarmed me. I'd accepted Paige's way of life and was happy to fund it. As long as she gave me the same space and let me live my life as I pleased. And what made me happy was being in the office, working. I'd taken after my father and I loved working. Paige had called me a workaholic but she'd made it sound like a dirty word.

I'd tried to explain to her that my workaholism was what funded her extravagant lifestyle.

"What can I do for you?" I said.

"Nothing actually, I just called to remind you about my wedding," Paige said softly.

My muscles tensed. I should have been expecting it as she had been in a relationship with the same man since our divorce was finalized. "Wedding?"

She sighed. "I sent you an invitation ages ago, and even though you didn't reply, I assumed you'd definitely be coming."

"I didn't get it." Not a surprise since I'd told my secretary to shred anything from my ex-wife. In my defense, I'd harbored a lot of bitterness then.

"I'll send you a virtual card. The wedding is in a week's time Stephen. You are coming, aren't you?" she asked, sounding hurt.

"I'll be there and congratulations," I said. "Is Ezra still spending his days at the golf club?"

Her boyfriend, now fiancé came from a super wealthy family and had never lifted a finger in his life to work. He spent his days at the club and the weekends going on short vacations. He and Paige were a match made in heaven.

"Yes, and loving it. I like that I get to see him whenever I want," Paige said in a barb aimed at me.

That had been one of the reasons she had cited for the divorce. I was never there for her and she wanted a family man.

"I'm pregnant too," Paige continued. "I wanted to tell you first before you read about it somewhere."

"I don't read gossip rags," I muttered, and tried to ignore the pain rumbling through me.

Paige had always wanted a baby, but I wasn't the kind of father she wanted for her baby. She wanted a dad who would always be there.

It had hurt but I'd also recognized it as the truth. I'd have made a terrible father, just as my father had. He had spent his days and half his nights at work, building his empire, Creamy Creations. Every state in the country had at least five franchises of the bakery my father started.

He'd been a great businessman but a terrible dad. I was the same. I loved my work and I was good at it, but I was shit at relationships.

"Congratulations," I murmured.

"You could have that too," she said. "Life is not all about making money."

"Says the woman who loves spending it," I mocked gently.

"Work can never replace love. I wish you knew what you were missing," Paige said, pretending she hadn't heard what I'd said.

"I'm happy for you," I said.

We'd both been very good at ignoring what the other person said, if we didn't like it.

"Thank you. Be sure to check the invitation. I'd like it very much if you'd be there."

"Yeah, sure."

After we said goodbye, I tried to focus on my work again and failed. I glanced at the time. Ten o'clock. Paige's news had awoken my restless spirit. I was genuinely happy for her and there was no doubt in my mind that our divorce was the best thing that had ever happened to us.

But like every other man, I hated failing and I had failed at marriage. It also jarred me that she thought I was living a less fulfilled life because I wasn't in a relationship. Work filled that hole for me and when I craved a woman's company and sex, there were plenty of them willing to play that role.

The phone on my desk rang and I reached for it with a frown. My secretary knew better than to interrupt me before eleven.

"Yes?" I barked into the phone.

"Your mother is here to see you," Eileen said, unmoved by my tone. She had been with me for almost a decade and was used to my bad moods.

"Let her in," I said with a sigh. My mother believed that it was her right to come into my office any time she wanted to without a warning call.

I got up as soon as the door swung open and crossed the room to kiss her cheek. "Hello Mother."

"Hello to you," she said, glancing around my office as though seeing it for the first time. "Are you sure you don't want to take your father's old office? He'd have loved for you to take it, plus it would be nice for me to see you all the time."

"You're hardly ever there," I point out. The thought of being an office away from my mother made me shudder.

"Maybe I would be if you were there. Besides, wouldn't it be easier to run the business from downtown?" she said as she lowered herself to the chair I had pulled out for her.

We'd had that discussion before. The only reason my mother wanted me close to her was so that she could introduce me to her friend's single daughters. Since my divorce, she had made it her life's mission to find me a wife.

"I told you Mother, my own business has to continue. Creamy Creations doesn't need me full time. Being here works well for me. My team members are all here and I can't move them downtown."

She raised her hands in mock surrender. "Okay, calm down. Let's talk about more important things, like the reason I came by. I've invited a few friends for dinner tomorrow night and I'd like you to be there."

She phrased it like a request but knowing my mother, it was an order. If my mother had been in the army, she would have made it to General with her bossy manner.

"Sure," I said and a look of surprise came over her features. She had expected a fight and any other time, I'd have said no but I'd learned to pick my fights with my mother.

I had a more important issue I needed her to agree to and I was sure she would give me a hard time about it.

"Great," she said and reached for her purse on my desk. "I'll see you tomorrow at seven then."

"Before you go Mother, there's something else we need to talk about," I said.

She settled back in her seat.

"The Creamy Creations on Elm Street."

Her features went still. It was a sore point between us and had been since she had franchised it to some woman who had previously run her bakery from home. Not our usual type of candidate for our potential franchisers.

"Yes, what about it?" my mother said, her voice tinged with wariness.

She was super protective about that woman and I'd never figured out the reason why. I'd left my mother to oversee Creamy Creations since we lost Father three years ago. But in the last two years, we'd started to lose our edge with reduced profits and market share and I'd stepped back in.

I was horrified by what I learned. My mother made decisions based on her emotions, which was a big weakness in business. We had a quality team that ensured all the products which carried our brand name maintained the high quality my father had set.

But even with a system in place, you had to be hands-on and physically visit the franchises every so often. It was my fault. I should have recognized my mother's waning interest in the business ever since my father passed on.

"We need to shut it down," I said softly, knowing the emotional attachment she had to the small bakery. "It's the only one of our franchises which is making a loss."

It was our smallest outlet and the very first one that my parents had started with. In those days, Mother was heavily involved with the business but as it became more successful, she took on a less active role.

"We can't shut it down," she said. "It means everything to me, and not just for sentimental reasons. The young woman who owns it is very hardworking and she deserves a chance, which is what we are giving her."

"Emotions have no place in business," I said.

My mother's face hardened. "Maybe in your world Stephen but in mine, compassion does."

"This is exactly why I didn't want to get involved. When I agreed to come on board, you promised to give me a free rein and run the business as I see fit."

The hard, uncompromising look left her face. "Please Stephen. This is very important to me. I have faith in Maria and I know she'll make it. She just needs time."

I could see that she was determined to hold on to the franchise. Still, I hadn't become one of the biggest venture capitalists in the country for nothing. The key to business was to know when to back off, push harder and when to compromise. This situation demanded the latter.

"Three months is all I'm going to give her," I said.

"Six months," my mother said. "You of all people should know that it takes time for a start-up to start making money."

Not when it was our franchise which was the reason why entrepreneurs preferred to operate under a known brand rather than starting from scratch.

"You could make it easier for her to succeed by helping her," my mother continued. "Her baking is perfect as is her set up. The only thing lacking is the marketing side."

My answer was a flat no but as always, I gave it a second thought before voicing it. It would be in our best interest as a company if I gave her some help. I wasn't an ogre and really did want her to succeed. If she did, so did I.

"Fine, I'll go and see if there's anything I can do," I said.

Our marketing efforts concentrated more on our brand rather than the individual outlets. The outlets had a responsibility to market themselves as well, which from what I'd seen the Elm Street Bakery did very little of.

"Thank you," my mother said. "I know Maria will appreciate it too."

I walked her to the door and before she left, she reminded me of the following evening's dinner. As much as I dreaded it, an hour or two was worth it just to get her off my back for the next couple of weeks.

MARIA

I was hunched over my computer trying to make sense of the figures in front of me. My father liked to say that data told the whole story. He was right because in my case, the data was telling me that once again, I had barely broken even for the month.

I couldn't afford to pay my overheads, that's all and leave a little for my living expenses which were very minimal. I lived in the apartment above the bakery and it came with the bakery. I knew what my problem was. Susan, the brand owner of Creamy Creations had gently pointed it out to me.

I loved baking and could happily hibernate in a kitchen for months as long as I had all my ingredients. I also wanted to be an entrepreneur and one trait that I needed to develop was the ability to switch from the creative to the business mode. Except that I didn't know how to.

Deep down, I believed that if my products were good, the customers would come. They did, but not nearly enough of them to raise my profit margin. Susan was an awesome human being but I also knew that she had her limits. More so now that her son had started taking a more active role in the business.

Nausea rose up my throat as it always did when I thought about the possibility of shutting down my little bakery. It had been my dream for so long to move the bakery from the basement of my apartment to a physical location where I could have walk-in clients.

The sound of someone clearing their throat brought me back to the present. I looked up to see Beth standing at the door.

"There's someone asking for you," she said, a look of nervousness on her features. "I think it might be Mr. Cohen."

My blood turned to ice. My worst fear was coming true. I swallowed a flood of saliva and rose to my feet. I just had to find a way of convincing him that the bakery would start showing a profit soon.

I smiled reassuringly at Beth and then followed her out. The smile froze on my face when the man staring at the goods on the counter looked up. The sight of him jolted something in me, as if I'd met him before but of course I hadn't. I wouldn't have forgotten such a beautiful man.

He had thick wavy hair that begged me to thread my fingers through it. My mind had gone out of control. My body had taken over and what I felt was intense awareness shooting through me. I'd never felt such instant attraction for a man and I fought the urge to flee. To return to the safety of the kitchen.

I raised my gaze from his muscular chest, a chest that made me want to fold myself against it and met cold, dark gray eyes. Eyes that resembled a storm. Eyes that jerked me back to the present.

"Is it always this empty in here?" he asked in clipped tones.

And just like that, my attraction evaporated and it dawned on me that I was dealing with an enemy.

"This is our slow hour," I said in equally clipped tones. I went to him and struck out my hand, impressed by my coolness when inside I was a frightened mess.

"Successful bakeries don't have slow hours," he said as he took my hand in a firm grip.

To my embarrassment, heat enveloped me, snaking over my body from the point of contact. I snatched my hand back as soon as I decently could.

"My name is Maria Swan," I said and forced my stiff lips into a smile. This man held my future in his hands and it was in my best interest to charm him, no matter how arrogant I found him.

He nodded. "Stephen Cohen."

"Do you want to come into my office," I asked him and without waiting for an answer, I whirled around and marched off.

Successful bakeries don't have slow hours. His words played on repeat in my head, mocking me. How dare he? I tried to hang on to my indignant anger but it soon ebbed away when it dawned on me that Stephen had not been wrong.

We had loads of slow hours and it had all to do with my lack of marketing skills. I sank into my chair and faced him, my heart pounding furiously and my top clinging to my sweaty back.

I'd been so excited to finally move the bakery from my apartment basement to a commercial space. It could be over in the next couple of minutes. I could make it a success if only the cold, arrogant man seated in front of me would give me a chance.

"Your bakery is our least profitable franchise, by a long shot," he said blankly.

My heart dropped to my feet. I wasn't averse to begging if it was going to work.

"Sad as it's where it all began." He glanced around my small office and scrunched his nose as if he could smell something that had gone bad.

He trained those dark gray eyes on me and my legs turned to jelly. I was glad I was seated because for sure, my knees would have buckled under me.

"My idea is to do away with it but my mother won't agree for sentimental reasons. That's a weakness in business," he continued.

The meaning of his words penetrated my brain and I said a silent thank you to Mrs. Cohen. She and I had bonded in a special way and she'd narrated to me how she and her late husband had struggled to keep the business afloat. She had brought me to tears with her encouragement.

"Six months is all I'm giving you," Stephen said.

I let out a breath I hadn't realized I'd been holding. "Thank you."

"What are you going to do differently in those six months?" he said, boring his eyes into mine.

A surge of heat raced through me and settled between my legs. I tried to feel disgusted with myself and failed. All I could think about was how it would feel to kiss those lips and feel his hard body against mine.

I'd definitely gone too long without a man if Stephen Cohen, of all people was getting me that hot.

"I'll do more marketing," I said weakly. I couldn't think with him looking at me like that. As if he could see into my soul.

He stared at me. "What kind of marketing?"

I stammered by way through an explanation but I could see from his expression that he was not impressed. Neither was I to be honest.

"In other words, you don't have anything planned?" he said.

I felt the way I'd felt when I was summoned to the principal's office for some misdemeanor I'd committed.

"I have a few ideas," I mumbled. I was crap at business.

Stephen cocked his head to the side and contemplated me. "I'm assuming that you have a ticket for the Event Planning conference this weekend?"

I stared at him blanking. I had no idea what he was talking about. "I haven't heard about it."

"Are you serious? It's the largest conference in the state and it's held every year. Every baker worth their money attends it. More importantly so do wedding planners and event companies. These are people you need to be networking with. Custom orders bring in a lot of money," Stephen said.

"I know," I said. If I'd felt like a failure before, now it was ingrained in me.

He stood up. "I promised my mother that I'd help you and I will. Be ready at eleven on Saturday. You live above the bakery, right?"

I nodded and jumped to my feet. I should have been grateful that Stephen had a spare ticket and was willing to take me. Instead, resentment bubbled inside me. He had come into my bakery with a condescending manner and then proceeded to tear me down.

But my ambition was bigger than my pride. I was a lot of things, including a terrible business woman but a fool, I wasn't. Going to that conference and networking with potential clients was the nudge I needed to start marketing the bakery better.

I walked him to the door of the office and said goodbye. It would have been more polite to walk him to the front door of the bakery but I didn't want to be polite. And I didn't like how he was making me feel. Resentment, aroused, angry, excited. I was relieved to shut the door behind him.

I'd just turned the lock when my sisters, Amber and Linda, showed up on the other side of the door. I pushed it open.

"Look at the sign, we're closed," I said, holding the door open.

"We're in need of something sweet, preferably with loads of cream," Amber said.

I laughed. "I've got plenty of leftovers for you to pick from before Sam comes for them."

Sam was a friend who ran the local food shelter and we had an arrangement where he came for the leftovers every other evening.

I hugged each of my sisters in turn. Amber was the oldest of the three of us, followed by Linda and then me. I shut the door, and took them to the kitchen where I'd been busy packing leftovers.

They both settled for banana nut muffins and I made them some coffee to go with it. We settled around the central table with our coffee as we usually did every single Wednesday after work.

"How was your day?" I asked Linda. She was a social worker and married to her job.

"Rough, but what's new," she said, stuffing a huge bite of the muffin into her mouth. "I had to place a five-year-old boy into foster care after months or even years of abuse from his mother."

Amber and I made sympathetic noises. Linda's job, while worthy was tough and it took a toll on her.

"I'm never going to get married or even have kids," she said hotly.

"Hey, not all parents are like that," Amber said. "Jack and I will make great parents, when we get children," she added, a sad tone in her voice.

I didn't ask but I guessed that the latest pregnancy test had come up negative too. Amber and Jack had been married for three years and in all that time, they'd tried unsuccessfully to have a baby.

The next step was IVF but the cost was prohibitive and they would have to save up for years. That was another reason why I needed the bakery to be successful. I'd be more than happy to pay the money they needed to get IVF done. I'd have done anything for my sister to be happy.

Amber worked in a beauty salon as a hairstylist and she had dreams of opening her own business but that was after she got the baby that she and Jack wanted so much. Our parents were retired and what they had was just enough for them. I was the only one who had a chance at making decent money to help them.

"How was yours?" Amber asked me.

"Good. Scary," I admitted and told them about Stephen's visit.

"He's right though," Amber said. "We all know how much you hate the business side of it, but you're an entrepreneur and marketing comes with the territory."

"I know," I said miserably. "That's why I agreed to accompany him to the Event Planners conference this weekend."

"Is he hot?" Linda said. "If you're not interested in him, you can throw him my way. I need good sex."

I rolled my eyes and Amber burst out laughing. "He's hot all right, but arrogant and definitely not your type of man. Not mine either for that matter." My face heated up when I remembered how my body had reacted to him.

To distract myself from thoughts of Stephen, I talked about the conference and what I was hoping to get out of it. I was excited about Saturday but only because it could be the missing piece to turn my bakery around. Not because of seeing Stephen again.

STEPHEN

In all the years I had lived in my apartment, I'd never stood for more than a minute in front of the mirror in the room sized closet. Usually, a cursory glance was enough to reassure me that I was decently dressed.

I found myself staring critically at my reflection before I had to go and pick Maria up. I'd thought of nothing else since our meeting in her bakery. Her big green eyes and perfectly heart-shaped face, framed by silky red hair held in a ponytail.

The smattering of freckles across the bridge of her nose and dimples that formed when she smiled. Yeah, she was hot and sexy. And naïve and innocent. Definitely not my kind of woman.

I loved my women sophisticated and wild between the sheets. I didn't need innocent ones like Maria. So why did I care how I looked as long as I was decent enough. With that, I stepped away from the mirror and grabbed my jacket. The event was kicking off at eleven and it was ten, a good time for me to leave.

I grabbed my car keys and left the apartment. I rode the elevator to the basement and strolled across the near empty parking lot to my car. Chicago traffic was light at that hour and in twenty minutes, I was sliding the car into a street parking lot in front of the bakery.

I made for the side door and rang the bell. A buzz sounded and I pushed the door open. The building was old and the stairs creaked as I went up, taking two at a time. I got to the landing and found Maria's front door open. I knocked lightly before I pushed the door open the rest of the way.

I stepped in just as Maria was grabbing her purse from the table. She looked up and our gazes met. The click of attraction I'd felt when we first met turned into a current of electricity that zapped between us. I hadn't imagined the mutual attraction.

I let my gaze ripple over the lines of her body. She looked amazing in a silver dress that hugged her curves in all the right places. Her fiery red hair fell down to her shoulders in gorgeous cascades.

I forced myself to remember that this was strictly business. That didn't mean that I was blind either. It was impossible not to let my eyes take in her full breasts or to ignore the pulse of my cock in my pants.

"Hi," she said breathlessly.

"Hi, you look beautiful," I said.

Her cheeks reddened proving my first impression that she was naïve and innocent. I can't remember the last woman who blushed when I complimented her.

"Thank you," she said. "I'm ready."

"Business cards?" I asked her.

She beamed. "Got them."

"Then we're ready." I held the door open and let her walk ahead of me. As she went past, my eyes were drawn to her cute, shapely ass and I pictured my hands cupping it and pulling her against my erection.

I followed her down the stairs and out onto the street. Outside, I rested my hand on the small of her back and led the way to my car.

"You don't have to do that," she said when I opened the car door for her.

"I want to," I said. "I was raised a gentleman."

She stared at me and then wordlessly entered the car. Her floral perfume lingering in the air even after she'd shut the door. I went around to the driver's side and got in.

"Anything I need to know about today's event?" she said.

"Meet as many people as you can and be sure to take their cards and give them yours," I said.

After meeting Maria, I understood my mother's protectiveness over her. Despite the flash of anger that came into her eyes when you so much as criticized her business, she was a good person and from what I'd seen, very hard-working. It was easy to find myself rooting for Maria Swan, just like my mother had done.

The only difference between my mother and me was that I wasn't ruled by my emotions. I made decisions based on facts and if Maria's bakery had not turned a profit in six months, she was out. No matter how hard-working she was. Creamy

Creations existed to serve its customers delicious goodies *and* to make a profit.

"Thank you for asking me to go with you," Maria said in her sweet voice that could coax a lion out of its den.

"You're welcome." Did she have a boyfriend or had she just gotten out of a relationship? Clearly, she wasn't married and if she had a boyfriend, I'd seen no signs of one.

We got to Hotel Iris where the event was being held. I brought my car to a stop at the entrance and handed my car keys to a valet. Maria was quite tall and came up to my neck, which was a first as I towered over most women, at six feet. I found myself wondering how it would feel to kiss a woman who was almost as tall as I was.

I gave our tickets at the entrance and we were shown in. I'd deliberately picked that hour when the long queues were gone. We entered the ballroom where the main conference was being held as a speaker was giving their talk.

Maria and I found seats at the back and settled in. The magic in those conferences was not the topics or the speakers, but in the people you met during breaks. I snuck a glance at Maria's profile. She really was a beautiful woman and it would have been a surprise if she was single.

The speaker finished his talk half an hour later and after ten minutes of question and answer, it was time for a break until the next session. I knew several people as I'd been attending the conference for years on behalf of my parents. I took Maria around introducing her to as many people as I could.

People who could elevate her bakery to the big leagues.

"Stephen! I've been looking everywhere for you."

I turned around at Ava's voice and beamed at her. I kissed both of her cheeks. "Ava, what a pleasure. It's been too long."

"I know. Busy, busy," she said, her eyes shifting to Maria. Ava owned one of the largest events management outfits in Chicago.

"I want you to meet someone," I said, turning to Maria. "This is Maria Swan. She's our newest franchisee and don't quote me," I lowered my voice dramatically. "But her cakes are the best."

Maria and Ava shake hands.

"It's a pleasure to meet you," Maria said warmly.

"Do you bake cakes for events?" Ava asked her. I'd never vouched for any particular bakery under our umbrella brand and Ava knew it.

"Yes, we do," Maria said, smoothly fishing out her business card and handing it to Ava. She gave a short pitch of her products that was just enough to garner Ava's interest but not long enough to bore her.

"That was perfect," I said to Maria when Ava left. "You're a natural marketer, you just need to get out more."

Her face flushed with pleasure and when she smiled, dimples formed on her cheeks. I momentarily forgot everything including where I was as I stared into her eyes. When she smiled, her whole face lit up. I wanted that smile directed at me while I was holding her in my arms.

Preferably in my bed with no clothes between us. Her nipples digging into my chest and her pussy...Fucking hell. I'd never been so hot for a woman. As if she could see into my filthy mind, her smile faded and she stared at me with her wide innocent eyes.

I tore my gaze away and took her arm, leading her to someone else I wanted to introduce her to. We worked the room but my concentration was gone. I did it all on autopilot. I couldn't get the image of Maria naked and writhing under me out of my head.

We listened to a couple more talks and in the evening, we mingled some more and then it was time to leave.

"I've never had such an exhilarating day," Maria said as I entered the car. "I can't believe how many people I met today. Potential customers."

My gaze dropped to her mouth and lust burned into my brain. "You did well. I'm very proud of you. I'd pegged you as the shy type with strangers."

She laughed. "No one in my life has ever accused me of being shy."

I didn't want to part from her company just yet. "Do you want to go for a drink to celebrate?"

I regretted my words as soon as they were out of my mouth. Going for a drink with Maria was a classic example of mixing business with pleasure. If it was any other business associate, it would have been okay. But I'd spent the whole fucking day fantasizing about her. Imagining what she would taste like and if she was quiet or wild in bed.

Things that were none of my business.

I hoped that Maria would say no to my invitation.

"I'd love that!" she said. "I'm too wired up to go home and Keziah is shutting down the bakery today."

"Do you have someone else who helps with the baking?" I asked her to get my mind away from the gutter.

"Yes, his name is Peter but he's not full time. He comes four times a week," she said.

"You'd better start thinking of employing him on a full-time basis," I said.

"Why?"

"I have a feeling that good things will come out of this." I'd put in a very strong good word for her and Ava in particular had promised me that she would try Maria out with a few custom orders.

"That would be so awesome," she said.

I drove us to my favorite cocktail bar and found a parking space in a street parking lot in front of the building. I loved it because they did light dinners as well and apart from nibbling only finger food at the conference, we hadn't really had a proper meal.

Inside, we were shown to a table in a nice quiet corner and as soon as the hostess left, Maria leaned across the table.

"Do you think I'll get in trouble for removing my shoes? It feels heavenly to finally get them off," she said, laughter in her eyes.

She was a different woman from the one I'd met at the bakery a couple of days ago. She'd probably understood what the conference meant for her business. And maybe she knew now that I wasn't an enemy. Her success was my success after all.

"I don't think they'll care, especially if you have pretty feet," I said, enjoying the banter.

She glanced down. "I might be biased but I think they're okay."

I did something I'd not have done if only I'd have given it a second thought. I reached under the table, took her right foot and placed it on my lap. I massaged it as I studied it.

"Gorgeous," I murmured. I meant it too. She had painted her nails a scarlet red color which looked risqué and sophisticated.

She let out a nervous laugh. "Thank you." She pulled her leg away and dropped it down to the ground.

"Here are your drinks and dinner menus," a server said, breaking the sexual tension between us.

I watched Maria over the top of the menu as I perused it. Her eyes were on the menu and she was biting down on her lower lip as though she was in deep thought. I was sure that she was feeling the current of attraction between us and it was making her as uncomfortable as it was making me.

Tonight was one night where I was going to have to exercise my self-control. Nothing was going to happen even though the chemistry between us could light a fire. We were going to have a nice dinner to celebrate the day and then I'd drop her home and each of us would continue with our lives.

MARIA

I was feeling careless and wild. The last time I'd felt like that had been when I graduated from college. Youth and hormones had been to blame then. The two glasses of wine I'd had after dinner were to blame this time. Not quite true, I thought to myself as Stephen and I walked to the car.

I couldn't deny it any more. I was attracted to Stephen. And not just any casual attraction for an attractive man that women felt every so often. No. It was raw attraction. A bonfire of lust that was consuming me with every minute I spent in Stephen's company.

He had beautiful full lips and I wanted them on me. I was glad that it was dark in the car and he couldn't see the rise and fall of my chest.

"That was a perfect day," Stephen said.

I'd seen the way he'd been looking at me over dinner. As if he wanted to eat me for dessert. And the worst thing was that I wanted him to. Shame and desire mingled through me. I couldn't wait to get home and slip between the sheets and forget Stephen Cohen.

"I had a wonderful day too," I said. "I'm excited for the future of the bakery." I couldn't think of business when my mind was consumed with lust. Just a few more minutes until you get home, I said to myself.

Relief and regret mingled when Stephen brought the car to a stop in front of the bakery. I slipped my shoes back on and grabbed my purse.

"Do you want to come in for coffee?" I blurted out. What the hell was wrong with me? Inviting Stephen into my apartment was asking for trouble. I couldn't be trusted around him. Not when it was late at night and I'd had a couple glasses of wine.

"Yes," he said, his voice husky. "I'm not ready for the night to end."

Was he flirting with me? "There's parking at the back." That sounded as if I was inviting him to spend the night, which I most definitely was not. "It's safer."

"Okay." He drove us around to the back of the building.

Stephen turned off the car and the air between us became charged again. He came around to open the door for me and as I got out, I brushed past him and pinpricks of awareness lit up my skin.

He placed a hand lightly on my back as we made our way to the front of the building. Was I really inviting Stephen up to my apartment when just days ago, I thought he as an arrogant prick? With trembling fingers, I fished out my keys from my purse and inserted them into the lock.

Stephen took over and held the door open for me. Being a gentleman seemed to come naturally to him. I liked it. I'd never dated a man who opened doors for me. Yeah, I know. My taste and choice in men had been terrible.

We were silent on the way up until we got to my apartment. I flicked on the light and watched as Stephen went to the sofa, sat and made himself comfortable. I felt like the guest and he the owner of the house.

"I'll go make the coffee," I said with a slight stammer.

"Don't," Stephen said, his eyes locking onto mine. "Come and sit by me first."

I'd no doubt what the invitation meant. Don't, a voice screamed in my head. My legs moved of their own accord and a second later, I found myself sinking into the space he had been patting. My heart pounded hard in my chest as I angled my body to face him.

"I don't know what it is about you Maria," he murmured and reached out to tuck strands of hair behind my ear. "You captivate me and I can't stop thinking of you."

My insides trembled. His words and his voice held me captive. I wanted him to tell me more sweet things. I ignored the voice in my head trying to reason with me. Men like Stephen knew exactly what to say to get women to do their bidding.

I wanted it too, my brain screamed. That thought shocked me. Inviting Stephen to my apartment, that was what I'd had in mind but hadn't been ready to admit it even to myself.

Instead of returning his hand back after tucking my hair, Stephen caressed my cheek and edged closer so that his breath fanned my face. I was sure that I'd stopped breathing. Close up, he was even more handsome. How was it possible that a man could be created so perfectly?

My hand shot out to touch the contours of his face.

"I want to kiss you so badly," he said. "But I need you to give me the go ahead."

I inhaled sharply. Another first. No man had ever asked for permission to kiss me. It was hot. And it made me feel powerful. Would it be so wrong to kiss him? Just once. Just to satisfy the craving for him that had taken over my body and turned me into a woman I hardly recognized.

"Kiss me. "

He brought his lips down, touching mine with surprising gentleness. His masculine cologne enveloping me as his mouth grew more insistent. A moan filled the air before I realized that it had come from me.

The kiss deepened and so did the heat enveloping my body. Somehow, we had moved closer to each other and my fingers were threading through his hair. The kiss was hard, then soft and then hard and demanding again. Just the way I'd imagined his kisses to be. Better.

Then he pulled away and I made noises of protests.

"I want you, Maria. I want to taste you and hear you moan and scream," Stephen said.

My insides turned to water. Every part of my body ached for him. My nipples became sharp points under my dress. I wanted his mouth on them, sucking and licking. Help me

God but I wanted him so desperately. No man had ever affected me physically the way Stephen Cohen had.

I knew he wasn't going to make another move until I said yes. "I want you too."

He slid to his knees and placed his hands on my knees. He dragged my dress up all the way until my panties were exposed. He bent down to kiss my thighs and then he spread them apart.

"You smell like candy," he said. He reached up to the band of my panties and gave them a gentle tug.

I lifted my hips and he slid them down my hips and my legs, leaving me exposed for him.

"Move to the edge," he growled. "I need to taste you now."

My breath came out in pants as I slid down the sofa until I was perched at the edge. A shock of pleasure shot through me at the first touch of his tongue.

"Oh God," I screamed as my nerves roared to life. I gripped his head as his tongue tantalized and teased me. Groans rose up my throat and spilled out of my mouth.

"You taste so good," Stephen said in between licks.

I was too far gone to talk. I pushed his head back down in response. He chuckled and continued sucking and licking my most sensitive bits. I wasn't a virgin by any means but I'd never been with a man who knew his way around a woman's pussy so thoroughly.

Stephen did things with his tongue and his lips that I'd never had done to me. He alternated between feather light and heavy touches, and just when I thought I couldn't take it anymore, he pushed his tongue deep inside and fucked me with it.

I lost my mind. I felt myself hurtling towards an orgasm. Then convulsive waves came over me and I called out his name over and over again. I clawed and writhed like a woman who hadn't had an orgasm in years, which I hadn't.

"Oh God, yes," I cried as I gradually came down from my high.

I felt rather than saw Stephen stand up and the next thing I knew, his hands were sliding under me and I was being lifted into the air.

"This way?" he said.

"Yes," I said breathlessly. "It's a one-bedroom apartment. You can't go wrong."

He chuckled as he carried me effortlessly along the hallway. He paused in front of the bathroom and proceeded further down.

"Bingo!" Stephen said and gently deposited me on the bed.

He draped his body over mine and sealed my mouth with his. My body grew hot again. I ran my hands over his muscled back and shoulders. He had the body of an athlete. Compact and muscular.

I felt it then, hard and big, throbbing against my thigh. Too soon, Stephen pulled away from my lips and trailed kisses down my neck. He bit my nipples gently through the material of my dress.

"More," I said.

"The dress. I want it off," he said.

He got off me and pulled me up to a sitting position. Together, we whipped the dress over my head, leaving me only in a white lacy bra. I needed his mouth on my aching nipples and I reached back to unclasp my bra. I shrugged out of it and allowed myself to fall back on the bed.

He stared at my breasts hungrily before lowering his head and taking a nipple into his mouth. He thumbed the other and alternated between sucking and rolling a nipple between his fingers.

I groaned deeply as the ache moved from my nipples to my pussy. "I want you," I moaned.

He teased me a little longer and then got off the bed.

I watched him lustfully as he unbuttoned his shirt, eager to have that hot body over mine again. Realizing that I was staring at him, Stephen slowed down his movements, unclasping his belt and then pulling down his zipper.

Heat travelled my body as he pulled down his pants and stepped out of them. Next to go was his boxer briefs, but the angle of his body as he slid them down his legs meant that I could not see what I'd been dying to see. His cock.

He straightened up and I got a full view of his cock. It was a beautiful thing, bigger than I'd ever seen and jerking back and forth as though it had a mind of its own. He picked something from his pants and then moved towards me. I couldn't tear my eyes away from his huge cock.

My pussy throbbed for him. I as wet and ready for him. He brought the condom packet to his mouth and tore it open. My mouth practically watered as he removed the condom and slid it down his length. His cock was so thick, he could barely fit the condom over it.

"There," he said when he was done.

He climbed between my legs and pushed my knees against my chest. Arousal juices seeped out of my pussy, down my thighs. He wedged himself between my thighs, spreading them apart.

He rubbed the tip of his cock around my entrance, teasing me and I arched my hips, a step away from begging him to fuck me.

STEPHEN

I shouldn't have studied her so hard, after all, ours was only going to be for one night. However, I found myself paying attention to every gasp that Maria made, every cry she uttered and every time she gripped the bed headboard tighter.

She looked so gorgeous lying on the bed, panting as if she couldn't catch a breath with her green eyes half closed. I loved the sounds she was making with every deep thrust.

"Oh God, you feel so good," she said. "Please don't stop."

"No chance," I said, pausing to get my control back. Her pussy clenched against my cock like a vise.

"Deeper…harder," Maria said.

Fuck. I had to distract myself with thoughts of the day to stop from coming right there and then. The combination of innocence and an expressive mouth was intoxicating. I fucked her harder and faster, and watched her face as her eyes rolled to the ceiling.

I was going out of my mind with the need to come, something that had never happened to me before. I'd been aroused all fucking day at the conference and in the bar. I'd thought of this moment but my dreams hadn't come close to the reality of how it would feel to sink my cock into Maria's sweet, hot pussy.

Beads of sweat trickled down my face and chest. Maria's hands left the headboard and she rested them on my shoulders, not caring about my skin, slick with sweat. She dug her nails into my skin as the tempo of her breathing changed.

"I'm going to come. Oh God, yes," she cried and then bit down on her lower lip.

It was so hot watching her orgasm. She raised her hips and then her body started to convulse. My balls tightened in response and when she gave a deep cry, I gave in to my release and we came within seconds of each other. I came with so much force, it felt like a fucking hurricane had left my body and entered hers.

Reality came crashing into me minutes later when we were lying side to side staring at the ceiling. It was a new situation for me in so many different ways. For starters, I'd never had sex with a woman in her apartment. I always took them to my place where I'd be in complete control.

Had I been home, I would have immediately turned to my side and gone to sleep. Come morning I'd have gotten a cab for her and that would have been the end of it. Now, every instinct screamed at me to get up and leave. But my body said otherwise.

Sex with Maria had been unexpectedly explosive and I wanted more of it. It was still night, after all and the deal with myself had been one night only with her. If I left now, I'd forgo the enjoyment we could both have for the rest of the night, until morning.

It wasn't a difficult decision to make. I turned to face her and draped an arm around her waist. She exhaled, as if she had been waiting for me to make a decision and then inched close and lay her head close to my chest.

Her breathing grew heavier and within minutes, she had fallen asleep. It had been a long day and sleep was stealing over me. I drifted off to sleep with a smile on my face.

The next time I came to, something wet and hot was on my cock. My first reaction was shock and fear, until the memories of the previous night came to me. Maria. I peeled my eyes open and made out her form in the semi darkness. She was crouched between my legs with my cock in her hands.

Her hair and the darkness obscured her face from my view but I felt as she traced the outline of her lips with my dick.

"I thought that would wake you up," she said without stopping what she was doing.

"It's the best alarm clock that I've ever had," I said, settling back to enjoy the ride.

"Your cock is so hard," she murmured. "Like granite."

I chuckled. No woman had ever compared my dick to granite, but it was a close comparison. A rumble rose up my throat as she used her tongue on the length of my dick.

She swirled her tongue over the head, driving me crazy. "I'm so fucking hard."

"Is this helping?" she said.

"Fuck yes."

She took all of my dick into her mouth and made slurping noises as she sucked it. I rocked into her mouth, softly at first, but I soon lost control and fucked her mouth, hitting the back of her mouth every time.

The sweet suction of her mouth was too much but I didn't want to come. Not in her mouth. We only had this one night and I wanted us to orgasm together, like we had in the night.

I sat up and gently pulled her away from my dick. "I want you to ride me." I pulled her to sit on my lap and cupped her face. She was naked and her pussy dripped juices onto my thighs.

She had a sweet musky taste in her mouth and I couldn't get enough of her kisses. Our tongues swirled together as we explored each other's mouths. I kissed her one more time and moved my mouth to her nipples.

Maria let out a cry as soon as my teeth bit one pebbled nipple. I teased the other one with my thumb. "Beautiful. I love your breasts and how they react to my touch."

"I love what you do with your mouth and fingers," she said, her voice husky with desire.

My chest expanded with pleasure and power. For a man, there was no feeling like knowing that you were making a woman feel good and want more. No business deal came close to the experience of great sex.

I feasted on her breasts, exploring every part with my tongue and fingers. My cock jerked back and forth between us and Maria reached down to wrap her hand around it.

"I want this inside me," she said.

"I need to grab a condom," I said and shifted to reach my pants that were on the floor.

"Wait," Maria said. "Can we do it without? I've never done it without a condom. I want to feel all of you. The contours of your cock."

"Fuck." The only way I ever had sex without a condom, is when the lady and I had done tests to be sure we were both healthy and when she was safe, contraceptive wise.

It was tempting. "I'm safe too," I said.

"I'm on the pill," she added, cradling my dick in her hand. She raised her hips and dragged the tip along her wet slit.

Fuck! "That feels incredible."

Her breathing grew faster. "It does. I love how big your cock is. It makes me feel so filled up."

I made a decision. "Let's do it." I gripped her hips and lowered her onto my cock.

"Oh God," she moaned as my rock-hard cock pushed through her tight, wet pussy. "It feels so good."

I'd never felt so good in my life. It was unbelievable how it felt to have nothing between us. It was a little irresponsible and I knew I'd regret it come morning but at that moment, it felt as if Maria and I had become one person. I couldn't tell where my dick joined with her pussy. We had melded into one.

Maria leaned forward and placed her palms flat on my chest. I reached up to clasp her nipples, tugging them and moving them back and forth. She whimpered as she made circles with her hips.

I rocked upwards, reaching the depths of her pussy. I needed more friction and more heat. I wanted all of it at once. I held her hips again and lifted her off my dick until just the head was buried in her, and then slammed her down. She screamed.

"Oh my God, oh my God," she cried.

Our movements became feverish and frantic. "You look and feel incredible," I said, my eyes glued on her beautiful bouncing breasts. She was the sexiest woman I'd ever been with and I wasn't sure how I was going to stay away from her after tonight, but I would.

I had to. After Paige, I didn't do relationships. Every woman wanted children at some point. Paige hadn't when we were dating and during the first years of our marriage but later, she changed her mind. Then decided, all without consulting me that I would make a terrible father and I was not what she wanted for her baby.

Even now the memory of her words hurt.

"I don't want this night to end," Maria said, pulling me back from my thought with her words and rocking of her hips.

"I don't either," I said, gritting my teeth.

We fell into a sensuous rhythm and kept our eyes locked on each other as if to imprint the memory of this night into brains. She cried out at the peak of each thrust, her voice growing hoarser. She was growing exhausted.

"I want to fuck you from behind Maria," I said and pried her off my dick, which jerked back and forth in protest.

Maria went on all fours and I moved to kneel behind her. "You have a gorgeous ass," I said, patting her curvy cheeks.

"Thank you."

If I wasn't so aroused, I'd have laughed at her politeness. Instead, I gripped her hips to hold her in place and then thrust into her in one fluid movement. She whimpered and went limp.

"You okay sweetheart?" I said, pausing and praying my dick had not hurt her or gone too deep.

"Oh God, yes, I'm fine. More than fine. I've never felt this way before," she said. "I can feel you in my belly," she added in a disbelieving voice.

I chuckled. "That's a good thing, right?"

"It's the best," she said, breathlessly. "Now move. Fuck me. Hard."

I slammed into her hard, and each time, my hips felt like they were slapping her curvy ass. She had meat on her, which I loved on a woman and I enjoyed watching her ass jiggle with every thrust.

Maria's pussy started to spasm as she gasped and moaned my name as if she couldn't get enough of me.

"I'm going to come so hard," she said and it was all I could do not to come right there and then.

Her pussy walls rippled around me and I bit down on my lip hoping the pain would distract me from the desperate need to come.

"Yes, oh God yes," Maria said as her body rocked with an orgasm. I kept my hands on her hips as I pounded home, bursting into her and filling her with my seed.

"Fill me up Stephen," she said as I pumped the last of my cum into her.

"You're so fucking sweet," I said, breathing fast. I withdrew from her and pulled her to lie on my chest.

She didn't talk for a few minutes and I thought something was wrong. "You okay?"

"Very okay," she said. "It's been almost two years since I've been with anyone. Let's say I'm a little overwhelmed."

Two years! "Why so long? I'm sure it's not from a lack of men hitting on you."

"I guess I want to concentrate on my business. I didn't want any complications and disappointments," Maria said.

Relief surged through me. Maria had the same goals as I did. She didn't want a relationship either, which was just perfect.

MARIA

A distinctively masculine scent rose up my nostrils waking me up from my half-asleep state. I stared at the figure in my bed startled until it came to me. Stephen. The conference and then the bar and then my apartment. Oh God, what had I done?

I couldn't even blame alcohol. I had only had a few glasses of wine and I usually carried my alcohol well. I'd been led by my lust. Nothing else. Harsh rays of the sun streamed in through spaces in the drapes. I was a fool but what was new when it came to men?

The very man who could take away my dreams of making the bakery a success is the same man I'd chosen to sleep with.

Fuck me, Stephen.

My words, spoken in a moment of mad passion came back to haunt me. I was a different person in bed from out of it. I was so embarrassed to think that Stephen knew that side of me. I became uninhibited between the sheets and Stephen had turned out to be the best lover I'd ever had, hands down.

He stirred and I turned to face the wall. Maybe he would wake up and leave quietly. Then we could pretend that this had never happened. I stayed still and hoped that he could not hear the sound of my pounding heart.

He let out a slight cough and then went still. I clamped down on a giggle as I imagined what was going through his mind. My bedroom was tiny, with just enough space for a bed and a closet. Stephen probably lived in a penthouse, or one of those massive mansions where the really wealthy lived.

He probably thought he was caught in a bad dream.

Then he let out a deep breath and I knew he had remembered the events of the previous night. What did he think of me now? I'd practically begged him to come up for coffee. Did he think I was a desperate, horny, single woman? If he did, he would be correct.

But that was last night. It was broad daylight and I was back to my senses. Which meant that I never wanted to see him again. It would be too shameful to look into his eyes again. Memories of the night washed over me and heat quickly gathered between my legs.

His cock. My thighs trembled from the memory. My pussy was sore from too much action, but that didn't stop it from becoming soaking wet again.

He moved but I wasn't sure to which position until he placed his arm on my thigh and softly massaged it. I stiffened and stayed still and unyielding, determined to pretend I was asleep.

After a few moments, Stephen gently pulled me to lie on my back, doing it so gently so as not to wake me up. I fought a smile, but retained my determination to sleep through it until he got the message and left. I let out a soft grunt of sleep for good measure.

I held my breath as I waited to see what he would do next. I didn't have long to wait. The mattress shifted and seconds later, my legs were gently spread apart. What would he think when he saw how wet I was? Shame and desire mingled hot in my throat.

His breath fanned my pussy as he placed his hands on my pussy and spread it open. Oh God. I wanted to cry out and say his name. The uninhibited Maria was threatening to come out. I bit my lower lip in an attempt to keep her reigned in.

I almost did it too until his tongue came into contact with my clit. I let out a soft moan but quickly swallowed the rest of it and kept on pretending to be asleep. If he kept it up, I didn't know how long I could act as if I was asleep.

He teased my clit with the tip of his tongue, the movements so feather light, it felt as if the wind was touching me. I resisted the urge to raise my hips. My need for more friction grew but just when I couldn't take it anymore, he flattened his tongue and dragged it along my slit, driving me insane with need.

My hips rose up of their own violation, rocking against his mouth. He swirled his tongue around my clit and I didn't care to pretend to be asleep. I reached down to clamp his head down with my hands.

Pleasure shot through my body with every swipe and lick of his tongue. I struggled to get enough air into my lungs, as if I was drowning in pleasure.

"Don't stop," I said.

Stephen chuckled. "I thought you were asleep."

I was momentarily embarrassed that he had known that I was pretending all along. "Maybe I was," I managed to say.

He inserted a finger while keeping his tongue on my clit doing delightful things. Things that were taking me closer and closer to the edge.

"Your pussy tastes so good," Stephen said. "I want to do this all day."

His words reminded me that out time was coming to an end. Sleeping with him had been a huge mistake but when he was pumping his finger in and out of my pussy and making my body erupt in a fire of thunder works, it was difficult to regret my mistake.

It was our last moment together and I wanted both of us to enjoy it. I nudged him. "I want to feel you inside," I said. "Please."

"Whatever you say ma'am," Stephen said.

My pussy throbbed for him. He placed my legs on his shoulders and went to a kneeling position.

"You look so hot, so ready for me," Stephen said, staring down at my pussy.

It made me feel sexy to have him looking at me like that, spread open for him. "Fill me up with your big cock Stephen."

He hissed. "If you keep that up, I won't make it past the entrance."

My laughter died in my throat when he plunged into me, his cock searing like a hot rod. I met his driving rhythm beat for beat. He stretched my walls, filling me completely with his hugeness.

I clenched my teeth as sensations rippled through me. Within a few minutes, I was on the cliff and a second later, I was tumbling over the edge. I screamed and fisted the bedsheets as the orgasm tore through me.

Stephen's release followed and I felt him explode deep inside me.

"Oh God," I said over and over again.

~

"Is it okay if I use your bathroom?" Stephen said later, swinging his legs to the edge of the bed.

In the harshness of daylight, I couldn't look at him. "Sure. It's down the hallway." He'd probably never been in an apartment that didn't have an en suite bathroom.

"Thanks," he said and padded off.

Now what? I got up and slipped on a pair of panties, shorts and a t-shirt. The fact that it was Sunday, my one day off made things even more awkward. Had it been a work day, I'd have gotten up early, left him sleeping and headed to the bakery. As it was, I was stuck in my apartment until he left.

I went to the kitchen and turned on the coffee machine. As I waited for the coffee, Stephen's footsteps sounded and then he appeared in the kitchen. His hair was ruffled as if he had

47

come from running his fingers through it. I remembered how good it felt to touch it.

"Coffee?" I said, feeling self-conscious in my t-shirt and shorts. I tensed, hoping and praying that he would say no to coffee and just leave.

"Yes please," he said and joined me at the old wooden table that sat in the middle of the kitchen. "Black, no sugar."

"Got it." I busied myself with pouring our coffee and when it was done, I set the mug in front of him and sat down facing him at the table.

He took a sip and made appreciative noises. He glanced at me over the rim of his mug and my face heated up.

"That was a lovely night."

I swallowed hard. I didn't know what to say in response. We'd spent the night having wild sex. What did you say the following morning? "It was lovely for me too."

I gulped too much coffee and it went down the wrong way. I fought down the cough, trying to make it discreet. No luck. That made it worse and when I finally coughed to get the coffee out, I sounded as if I was drowning.

"Are you okay?" Stephen said, jumping from his chair and coming around to my side of the table. He whacked my back. Hard. The coffee dislodged and flew out of my mouth. To say that I was embarrassed was an understatement.

He was probably wondering how in God's name he had found me sexy the previous day.

"That was embarrassing," I said he sat back down.

"It can happen to anyone," Stephen said.

I couldn't imagine Stephen choking over his coffee or food. He was too sophisticated for that kind of clumsiness.

I carefully sipped my coffee again, this time ensuring that it went down the right way. I could feel Stephen's gaze on me. What was he thinking? Maybe how to gracefully leave my apartment. Or he was wondering how to tell me that last night had been a one off.

Panic came over me as I imagined that conversation. Compared to that, choking had not been embarrassing. If he gave me that little speech, it would kill me. I had to tell him first.

"So, about last night," I started, hoping my voice sounded normal. "Like I said, it was lovely but I don't want you to think anything of it or have expectations. I'm busy with the bakery now, as you can imagine. I have a lot of work ahead of me."

Relief drew itself on his features. I'd been right. He'd been bracing himself to give me that little talk. I was glad that I'd beaten him to it.

"No, it's fine and I'm glad you've told me. It's always easier when everything is laid on the table," Stephen said. "I'd still like to help you with the bakery. Maybe brainstorm some ideas."

"Sure, I'd like that very much," I said, a part of me relieved that I would see him again.

"I'll pop in one of these afternoons, when you're not busy," he said and downed the last of his coffee. He stood up. "Thanks again for a great afternoon and night."

"You're welcome. Thanks for inviting me to the conference," I said, following him out of the kitchen to the front door.

I mentally patted myself on the back. It was not uncomfortable to tell him goodbye. Not when there were no expectations. Had I not said anything, I'd have been wringing my fingers wondering if he would ask to see me again. Playing a mental game of will he or won't he.

I didn't want him to call and I definitely didn't want it to go further than that. Sex with him had been great...no, out of this world, but that was all either of us had to offer. I felt so mature and sophisticated as he kissed me goodbye at the door.

Until the door banged shut. Longing rose inside of her. Maria reminded herself that her life was rich and full as it was. She had no use for a man right now. She had the bakery which took up a lot of her time and energy. She had parents and sisters and friends.

Still, she couldn't help but wonder how it would feel to be in a good relationship again. To wake up against the hard, warm body of a man and to be surrounded by those masculine scents that were so intoxicating.

STEPHEN

"We started Ace Tech three years ago in Mike's living room," Jason said, gesturing at his partner seated on his right side.

There were five of us in the conference room. My team, made up of three guys and Linnet, and the two entrepreneurs who came into our offices to give us their pitch. They had impressed us with the numbers they had given us for the past three years and we liked the projections they had worked out.

Without warning my mind drifted to Maria. I hadn't seen her all week like I'd told her I would. Fear clutched at my heart whenever I thought about going by the bakery. I'd felt things that night that I had no business feeling. Being with her had been too different, too special.

I'd tried to look at her as any other woman I'd slept with, but it didn't work. I'd had the best day and night of my life. I fought down a chuckle as I compared the Maria I'd know at work and Maria in the throes of passion. The different faucets of her personality intrigued me and I wanted to get to know her more.

Peel more layers. But that wasn't going to happen. I had no place in my life for relationships or marriage. I had failed at it once and I wasn't going to try again. I wasn't going to experience the hurt I'd felt when Paige declared me unsuitable to become a father.

I recalled what she had said in the kitchen and wanted to laugh. It had been a first for me to have a woman tell me not to have expectations about us because we'd had sex. I'd finally met a woman who said it like it was.

"Do you have any questions, Stephen?" Linnet said.

I jerked back to the present. I didn't know how long I'd sit there daydreaming about Maria but I'd heard nothing of the last part of the presentation. "No, I'm fine."

I could feel Linnet and the guys' puzzled looks. I never not have questions to ask. I forced myself to listen as my team questioned the entrepreneurs. Usually, these meetings excited me. They were what made my work as a venture capitalist exciting and fun.

When the session was over, I excused myself and headed to my office. I shut the door behind me and folded the sleeves of my shirt, feeling uncomfortably warm. I knew it was me because the AC was permanently on in the office.

My cell phone vibrated as I sat down and when I glanced at the screen, my chest tightened. Ariana. Why was she calling me? I hated being pulled back into the past. I'd slept with her once only, and I'd regretted that once. I'd realized very quickly that Ariana was looking for a husband and I definitely was not in the running.

So I'd given her a similar speech to the one that Maria had given me that Sunday morning after we had sex. I'd thought that Ariana had taken it pretty well until she started calling me, begging to see me again. I'd made it very clear that I wasn't interested and she had finally left me alone.

That had been two months ago. I couldn't imagine why she was calling me now. I answered the phone.

"Ariana, how are you?" I said, trying to keep my voice friendly when what I wanted was to press disconnect before I even heard her voice.

"Stephen, hi," she said cheerfully. "I'm just around the corner from your office and I thought I'd pop in."

I inhaled sharply. We were back to that. Ariana had no luck. I'd dealt with persistent females throughout my life and there wasn't a single one whom I'd not dealt with.

It was time to be blunt. "That's not a good idea, Ariana."

"It's important. There are some things we need to talk about and we can't do it over the phone."

Her tone of voice had changed from flirting to a business one. I made a snap decision. The less time we wasted on the phone the better. I could afford to give her two minutes of my time. "Fine but only for a minute. I'm busy."

"You always are," she said. "I'll be there."

I disconnected the call and called my secretary to tell her that when Ariana came, she should show her in. I settled back to wait and sure enough three minutes later, she was being shown into my office.

I stood up as she entered. "Have a seat," I said when my secretary shut the door.

Instead of sitting down, Ariana came around my desk and went on tip toe to kiss my cheek. I swallowed down my irritation at her familiarity.

"It's so good to see you," she said as she sat down.

Ariana was beautiful by any normal male standards. The only problem with her was that she had a predatory manner about her, the one that women who were looking for marriage had. It put off men.

"Like I said, I have a pretty packed afternoon. What's up?" I said and stared at her.

She licked her lower lip. "I'm sure you do but when you hear what I have to say, you'll be so happy, you'll forget your busy life."

The only thing that would make me that happy was for her to leave and promise that I'd never see her again. My stomach muscles tensed in morbid anticipation but I kept my face neutral.

"I'm pregnant Stephen and you're the one responsible," she said.

I burst out laughing. "That's funny," I finally said when I recovered. "Because we only had sex once and we used a condom."

She glared at me. "This may come as news to you but condoms tear and having sex once doesn't preclude you from conceiving."

She was serious. Fuck. "I know that but, in our case, I know that the condom did not tear. I don't know what games you're playing at Ariana but I'm not the father of your baby. You need to search your memory again. You dialed the wrong number here."

She narrowed her eyes. I couldn't believe that I'd found her beautiful.

"What are you saying? That I sleep around?"

My muscles quivered with contained anger. I was losing my patience. "I don't care whether you sleep around or not. I just want you to drop this ridiculous accusation and get the hell out of my office."

"How dare you?" she hissed leaning forward. "I'd thought we could do this like civilized people and parent our child together. If you want to play it dirty, I can do that too. I'm sure the press will be very happy to hear my side of the story."

My anger dissipated as it dawned on me where this was going. Maybe she really did believe that I was the father but I was sure that I wasn't. The reason I was so sure was because I hadn't come that night. For some reason, I just hadn't been able to get into it with Ariana and that was one of the reasons why I hadn't seen her again.

So there was no way she was pregnant with my baby but the press did not know that. It was her word against mine and in such matters, the jury that was the public, took the woman's side.

If she had come to me several months earlier, I would have kicked her out of my office. Her timing was spot on. I was slowly becoming the face of Creamy Creations and I could not afford to be involved in a scandal.

Still, it irked me that she could just walk into my office and threaten me.

"What do you want?" I said to her.

"I want your support with this pregnancy," she said and tears filled her eyes. "I want you to be there for me. I want us to do this together."

I was fuming. "Money?"

Her eyes darkened. "I don't want your money. What I want is your time and support."

The bottom line was that she wanted money. And loads of it. I would happily give it to her and my support as well, if she was carrying my child, but she wasn't. I didn't know how to play this. She had me by the balls until she gave birth. Only a DNA test was going to get me off the hook.

What I needed was time to think and come up with a plan. Talk to my lawyer and find out my options. "Look, you've sprung this on me without warning. I need time to digest it."

Her features softened. "Are you excited, just a little bit? Can you imagine that? We've made a child together?"

I forced a smile. "It is exciting."

That seemed to satisfy her. She stood up. "I'll be waiting for your call. Don't make me wait for too long."

I got up and swiftly moved to the door before she got the idea to kiss me again. When she left, I shut the door and reached for my phone. I had my lawyer on speed dial and he answered on the second ring.

"Hey Jeremy," I said by way of greeting.

We exchanged pleasantries then I told him exactly what had transpired with Ariana.

"How can you be so sure that you're not the father?" Jeremy said. "Condoms do tear and you might not know it."

Fuck. Admitting to another man that you'd not ejaculated was a difficult thing but I had no choice.

"Oh," he said after I told him. "Is that a common problem you have because I know a good discreet doctor who can help?"

"I'm fine, thank you very much. It was just the one time. So you see, I couldn't possibly be the father of her baby even though the condom tore."

"I see that but it still leaves us in a vulnerable situation. You really need to play it cool here. You're only option is to convince her that you're not the father. Let her see how disastrous it will be for her when the DNA test comes out and you're proven not to be the father," Jeremy said.

"And just how do I do that?" I asked him.

Jeremy and I went back a long way. In addition to being my lawyer, he was a childhood friend. Our fathers had been close friends too.

"The same way you convinced her to enter your bed," he quipped and chuckled.

I sighed. "Fine then, I'll find a way. You're sure there's nothing legal we can do at this point?" I didn't want to have to deal with Ariana again.

"We can but whatever we do will attract media attention, which is what we're avoiding here."

After the call, my office felt cramped, as if the air had become stifled. I needed to get out to refresh my mind. I left the office with no destination in mind but as soon as I got out, I flagged down a cab and gave the bakery's address.

I'd promised Maria that I'd have a brainstorming session with her and it was as good a time as any. Most businesses slowed down in the afternoon and then picked up in the evening as people left work and picked up something to eat on their way home.

The cab dropped me in front of the bakery and as I got out, I glanced up at Maria's apartment and my cock swelled. A strong longing for a repeat session came over me. What would be so wrong about another passionate night like the one Maria and I had experienced.

There would be no harm as long as both of us knew our boundaries. And we did. Maria had articulated it very well when she said that her energy was on making the bakery a success. If she was for it, I would be happy to be used as a pleasure machine.

I entered the bakery and the first person I saw was Maria standing at the counter arranging a book on the side. She turned and when our eyes met, everything in me went still. I was hit anew by how beautiful she was. Her hair was held back in a simple ponytail and she had no makeup on.

She looked natural and fresh and good enough to eat. She smiled and my heart took off on a gallop in my chest. I had it bad for Maria. She made the caveman in me come out. I wanted to hoist her over my shoulder, carry her upstairs to her apartment and ravage her.

"Hey you," I said, going to where she stood.

I'd grown immune to the smells from bakeries having been is too many of them over the years but the chocolate scent coming from the muffins on the corner filled the air and made me want to sniff appreciatively.

"Hi," Maria said with a cool smile but I noticed that her cheeks were tinged with red. Was she uncomfortable at seeing me again or was she as aroused as I was?

An urge to touch her, even fleetingly came to me and I bent to kiss her cheek. She smelled of vanilla and chocolate. Her cheek was soft against my lips and it took all my self-control not to swoop in and kiss her on the mouth.

When I drew back, I noticed the look of surprise on her face. Pleased surprise.

"Sorry I haven't kept my promise of coming to brainstorm more ideas with you," I said. "It's been crazy busy at work." That was the truth though there was nothing new about that. It was always busy at work.

Entrepreneurs were always looking for funding and we were always looking for companies to invest in.

"It's okay. I was busy too. Ava called me and then came over. She gave us an order for this weekend. Two other potential clients called and made appointments," she said, her eyes gleaming.

"That's great news," I said, glad that Ava had come through.

"Do you want some coffee?" she said.

"Coffee would be great, thanks."

MARIA

Was he thinking about the last time I served him coffee in my apartment, wearing shorts and a braless top? I'm a mess. I can't imagine how my hair looks and my face is so hot, I'm sure he can tell how nervous his sudden appearance has made me.

I set two mugs of coffee on the table and take the chair opposite his. My heart beats so hard, I'm afraid that Stephen can hear it. I haven't seen him all week and, in that time, I managed to convince myself that once had been enough and there was nothing special about him.

Wrong. He was the sexiest male that had ever walked the earth. Just looking at his mouth was enough reason to start panting. The things he could do without mouth. An ache formed in the middle of my legs as the memories came over me. The ache grew to painful proportions.

It was as if in having sex with Stephen, a giant had been awakened. I squeezed my thighs together as the ache grew to unbearable proportions.

"Are you okay?" Stephen said. "Are you in pain?"

Then I engaged my mouth before my brain. "I ache." I clamped my hand over my mouth as soon as the words were out. Maybe I hadn't said that aloud, I thought in panic. Or maybe I could pass it off as a belly ache. Anything but the truth.

I was a walking embarrassment. Stephen's face told me that he'd not only heard it but he also understood what I meant. Oh God, I was going to die. I couldn't even have a decent conversation with him without shaming myself.

"Can we have this coffee upstairs?" he said, giving nothing away with his face or voice.

I wanted to say no and that he had misunderstood me. But I couldn't. I could already imagine what would happen if we went upstairs and I wanted it. Badly. All my baking was done for the day. I usually spent this time of day catching up with my paper work. I could disappear for an hour and no one would raise an eyebrow.

"Sure, we can go upstairs," I said, sounding like a realtor taking a potential client to a showing. "I'll just let Keziah know that I'm going out for a bit." I don't know how I managed to stand up and walk to the kitchen, but I did.

I trembled as I fished the keys to my apartment from my back pocket and gave Keziah some excuse about needing to go somewhere. Stephen was not where I'd left him and I experienced a moment of panic. Maybe he'd decided that I was dangerous and he didn't want to be around me.

A sex maniac who could not control her urges. I was worried for myself too. I'd always loved sex but I'd never found a lover who turned me on the way Stephen did. It was frightening to go back on my word to myself. I'd promised that ours would be a one-night stand only.

I caught a glimpse of him outside the bakery and with relief, I hurried out. There was nothing wrong to be turned on by a man. It just meant that I was a healthy young woman with normal sexual urges. What was wrong with having a little fun together? We were both adults and I'd already expressed to him my thoughts on a relationship and he agreed with it.

As long as we were enjoying ourselves, and hurting no one, there was nothing stopping us from having sex one last time. There was only one problem. I'd been hard at work all day and I badly needed a shower.

Stephen flashed me a smile and then we walked to the door that led upstairs to my apartment. I felt his gaze as I strolled up the stairs and I swayed my hips a little more than I normally would. I wished I was wearing something sexier than my work pants and blouse.

As I opened the apartment door, Stephen placed his hands on my hips, igniting the fire in my belly. My body shook with lust and all I could think about was that strong, hard body against mine.

I opened the door and staggered in, high on desire. Stephen followed me in and immediately pulled me into his arms and kicked the door shut. Urgent with need, his mouth found mine and we kissed feverishly. I roped my hands around his neck and pushed my body against his.

His cock, hard and erect, pushed against my thigh. I snaked a hand between us and cupped it over his pants. He groaned into my mouth as I squeezed his cock. His hands cupped my ass tightly, almost lifting me off the ground.

Shower. I needed the bathroom first before we could continue. I pulled away from his mouth and dropped my hand from his cock.

"I need a shower really badly," I said and wiggled out of his hold. I didn't give him time to respond and hurried off to the bathroom. I stripped off my clothes in record time, entered the shower and turned on the water.

My whole body was on fire and I stood under the water hoping that it would cool me down. The door squeaked and I opened my eyes to see Stephen strolling in buck naked with his cock jutting out of his body. It looked huge and intimidating and exciting.

"You didn't expect me to stand there waiting with this?" he said, and wrapped a hand around his cock.

"It's huge." It was one thing to see his cock in the night but to look at it in broad daylight…

He stroked it as he stood at the edge of the shower. "You act like you haven't seen it before."

"It was at night." I couldn't take my eyes off his hand as it moved up and down his cock. "That's so hot." I was panting like a wild animal.

"You do this to me," he said, his voice thick with lust. "Wash yourself."

I decide that it's sexier to use my hands rather than the washcloth and pour a dollop of shower gel on the palm of my hand. I inhale deeply and then rub it all over the top part of my body.

Beads of white liquid sprout at the top of his cock. As he moves he rubs his thumb over it, using it as lubrication. His eyes are on me as I rub the shower gel all over my breasts.

My nipples stood like two points on my chest, aching for Stephen's touch. I closed my index fingers and thumbs on both nipples and squeezed. A soft moan escaped my lips. Stephen pumped his cock faster.

I played with my nipples a while longer and then continued washing myself. I saved the best for last and dropped my hand between my legs and parted the folds of my pussy. I pushed a finger in and moaned loudly as a shot of pleasure shot through me.

The next thing I knew, Stephen was beside me, gently prying my finger out of my pussy. "You don't get to have all the fun alone."

"I haven't finished showering," I teased him.

"Now you have," he growled and lowered his head to take a nipple into his mouth. He sucked and licked it, tracing its outline with the tip of his tongue. He kept one hand wrapped firmly around my waist to keep me steady.

He scraped my nipple with his teeth, taking me to new heights of pleasure. I moaned and scraped his muscular back. I gasped and moaned as tension grew in my body.

I needed more. "Please Stephen, now."

He stood up and gently turned me around. Then he took my hands, raised them and placed them flat against the tiles.

"Tell me again what you want?" he said. "I love your dirty mouth, Maria. I got hard every time I remembered the things you said last Saturday."

I laughed softly, unembarrassed.

"Tell me," he urged.

I pushed my ass out and spread my legs. "I want your big cock in my pussy, fucking me, making me feel good."

He let out a sharp, loud breath. "You love it, don't you?"

His cock nudged the opening of my pussy. I closed my eyes as he slowly pushed it in.

"Oh God yes," I said as he filled me up inch by inch. How had I stayed so long without this?

Then it was all in and he was pulling out and then slamming back in again. I moved my legs back to give him better access and when he rammed into me again, I let out a scream.

"You feel so fucking good," Stephen said and then slapped my ass lightly.

With every thrust, he hit my sweet spot and I could feel by body coiling tighter and tighter as I hurtled towards an orgasm. Stephen gripped hips and fucked me harder and deeper.

I was glad that there was no other apartment near mine as I was sure that my screams could be hard from afar. My body tensed up as the orgasm drew nearer.

"I'm going to come," I cried.

I was beginning to crumble. I couldn't tell my right from my left. I fisted my hands and arched my back, pushing my ass out. "Oh God, yes." My pussy clenched around his cock and he let out a loud grunt.

I cried out his name as I exploded and seconds later, he said my name and filled hot cum inside me, creating a flood deep inside me.

"Oh my God," I said as I came down from my high.

MARIA

"Y"ou're late," my mother said as I stepped into the living room of my old childhood home.

Mom stood up and I went to her and hugged her. She was a petite woman which belied the fact that she was the one who steered the ship that was our family.

"Sorry Mom," I said as she drew back and cupped my face and studied it.

"You look tired," she said and dropped her hands.

"It's been a long day." My face heated up. I was sure that the way I'd spend my evening was written all over my face.

After the shower, Stephen and I had dried each other and then he started tickling me and we tumbled into my bed. One thing led to another and what had started as play, quickly became another session on my bed. After that, we'd taken another shower and parted ways, but not before he invited me to his place to talk about work.

That had made me want to laugh but I'd kept a straight face. Work indeed. The chemistry between us was out of this world and we could not be trusted to be alone in a house 'working'.

I'd said yes, but only because I was curious about him. I wanted to see where and how he lived. Okay, yes, I also didn't mind some more action. Who knew how long this thing between us would last and when it would end. I didn't know how long I would stay before getting some more action.

It was best to have as much of him as I could while we were both willing.

I kissed my father's cheek, hugged my sisters and Jack.

"I haven't seen you in forever," I said to my brother-in-law. He was a firefighter and a lot of times, he missed our dinners at my parents' house as it coincided with his shifts.

"I know," he said. "How's the bakery doing?"

"Good," I said as images of Stephen standing naked in my bathroom flashed in my mind.

What was the matter with me? I was obsessed with that man's body and sex with him. I was behaving like someone who had just discovered sex.

I felt that way too. Nothing could have prepared me for sex with Stephen. He made all the other men I'd slept with look like boys in terms of experience.

"We're starting to get really large custom orders, which is awesome," I said. "Good things are happening."

It must have been my imagination but I thought I saw Jack and Amber exchange a look that I could not interpret. Not that it mattered. I'd noticed a lot of married people had this secret language between them that made me long for someone of my own to do it with.

My thoughts meandered to Stephen again. If only we had met at the right time when both of us were free to get into a relationship. I gathered from our short conversations between having sex that he had once been married. He had said something in passing but I figured that his divorce had scarred him.

I idly wondered what his wife had been like. What sort of woman would a sophisticated wealthy man like Stephen marry? Definitely not a homely woman like me.

"Let's take this to the dining room please before my food gets cold," my mother said and we all stood up.

I offered to help her carry the food to the already set table. We held hands and said grace and then passed the food dishes around.

"Thanks mom," I said as I heaped roasted potatoes onto my plate. "Everything looks so tasty and smells so good."

"I'm surprised you can say that seeing that you're surrounded by yummy bakery smells all day," my mother said.

"Your own cooking doesn't smell quite as good," I said.

We chatted lightly over dinner with all of us giving a summary of the past week. My parents were retired but they busied themselves with charitable activities and golfing for my dad.

After dinner, Linda and I cleaned up and then joined everyone else in the living room for coffee.

"So, there's something Jack and I wanted to talk to you about," Amber said, wringing her hands on her lap.

I shot Linda a questioning look. She shrugged in response. Clearly, she had no idea either what it was all about. Jack took Amber's hand and squeezed it which made me think that it had something to do with the baby.

My heart squeezed painfully knowing that it could not possibly be good news. Amber would have already told us.

"We've decided to use a surrogate for our baby," Amber said.

Deafening silence followed her announcement. I scrambled my brain for what I knew about surrogacy. Expensive was the word that came to me.

"Isn't that expensive?" Linda said, voicing her thoughts.

"It would be but we're thinking of asking our family for help with this," Amber said. She exchanged another look with Jack.

"What do you mean?" I said.

"Well, I have two sisters and each of them can possibly carry a baby to full term," she said.

I stopped breathing as understanding dawned. I opened my mouth to say something and then promptly shut it.

"I hope you're not thinking of asking me," Linda said. "I'm too busy at work and really, I find the whole baby business distasteful."

My jaw dropped as I stared at Linda. My sister had no filter in her mouth but even that was a little too much for her.

"Linda," my mother snapped. "How can you say such a selfish thing? We are family and as such we do whatever we can for each other. Your sister has been wanting a baby for the longest time. We all feel her pain and if there's something we can do, we'll do it."

Silence followed my mother's outburst. I kept my eyes downcast. I could feel everyone's eyes on me.

"Maria," Amber said softly. "Will you do it for us?"

So many things raced through my mind and to my shame at the top of the list was Stephen. We were having so much fun together. If I were to agree to Amber's request, it would mean an end to that. No man was going to keep a lover who was pregnant and the baby was not his.

Then there was the bakery. Things had picked up considerably since the conference. If the order we had from Ava went well, she had promised all her business. As long as we delivered. I had other things planned which all needed my time and energy.

I was sure that pregnancy took a toll. What would happen to my business if I got pregnant and I couldn't continue working for whichever reason? Nausea rose up my throat as I thought about what Amber and Jack were asking of me.

I loved my sister with all of my heart and I wanted them to have a family and be happy. But being pregnant was a huge commitment.

"She's your sister Maria," my mother said.

"It's a lot to ask of someone," my father said, speaking up for the first time. "Give her time to think about it. She has her own life you know. A new business that is taking a lot of her time."

I could have kissed my father. Then I shifted my glance to Amber and the anguish in her eyes wiped away all my reasons for not wanting to help her. If I were to estimate, the whole business would take about a year. What was a year of my life if it would make my sister happy?

"Please think about it," Amber said. "It would mean the world to Jack and me."

I nodded and smiled reassuringly at her. "I will."

Another thought dawned on me. If I agreed to it, the first child I would push out of my body would be my sister's child. I would have to give that child away even though the baby would be theirs biologically.

I wondered how surrogate mothers dealt with that.

The rest of the evening was filled with tension and we couldn't go back to the easy camaraderie we usually enjoyed as a family. I was glad when the evening came to an end and Linda and I left together.

We didn't speak until I drove off.

"Are you seriously considering doing it?" Linda asked me.

"What choice do I have?" I said, irritated all over again at how quickly Linda had extricated herself.

"Of course you have a choice," she snapped. "Don't be a fucking martyr. I hate it when you're like that. If you don't want to do it, just say so, like I did."

I sighed deeply. "I want to because I know how much it will mean to them but there is so much going on in my life right now."

"Like what?" Linda said.

"Well, there's the bakery to start with. It's really picking up," I said. "Then there's my personal life. I have a lover."

"What?" Linda cried out. "You're not serious. Like a relationship?"

I shook my head. "Nothing like that. It's just sex but it's fun and I'm enjoying myself for the first time in years. If I agree to Amber's proposal that has to come to an end."

"Wow, you're a dark horse sis. Who is it? Wait, don't tell me. Let me guess. Stephen the millionaire."

I laughed. "More like a billionaire but yeah, he's the one. But neither of us wants a relationship and it's working out perfectly."

"I'll bet it is. Is he any good in the sack? I heard that rich dudes were terrible in bed."

"Wrong, if Stephen's anything to go by. He's great," I said.

"Say no then. Don't let mom and Amber pressure you into something you don't want to do," Linda said hotly.

"It's easy to say that but the fact is that she's my sister and she needs help," I said.

"She's my sister too but I think that's asking for too much. I've said enough times that I never want to have a baby, which means I don't want to get pregnant either and I'm glad I said no from the onset."

Part of me admired Linda for her capacity for selfishness. Linda wasn't a bad person but she never went out of her way for anybody and this situation was a classic example. She hadn't even given Amber's request a second thought.

"And I think you should say no too," she continued.

I couldn't stop thinking about the heartbreak I'd seen in Amber's eyes when she pleaded with me to think about it. She hadn't ever confided the details of their journey in trying to conceive but I knew what couples who couldn't easily get a baby went through.

I made a decision there and then. I was going to help my sister and her husband get a baby. No price was too high for their happiness.

"Do you think it's hard giving the baby away after it is born even though you know that it's not yours biologically?" I said.

Linda inhaled deeply. "You're going to do it, aren't you?"

I nodded. "I'd do anything for either of you."

"That's a sweet sentiment Sis but in this case, I think that you're a fool." Linda was silent for a few seconds. "They offer counselling. I think that helps."

STEPHEN

I was living a double life. How was it possible that I was trailing around Ariana in the baby store, pretending to be interested in what color of beddings she got for the cot. I'd seen the wisdom of Jeremy's advice but I didn't like it. I'd called Ariana and she'd asked me to take her shopping for the baby.

Her pregnancy was just a small bump but she was acting like she was going to give birth the following week. I'd invited her to buy anything she wanted and she was clearly taking me up on my offer. She was buying everything in sight. I didn't mind. Spending money did not bother me even though the baby was not mine.

What pained me that I was wasting my precious time with Ariana when I could be preparing for tonight's dinner with Maria. I was looking forward to cooking for her and spending a nice evening eating, talking and making love.

"I think that should do it," Ariana said and I followed her to the counter and gave my card.

"I'm glad you're coming around," Ariana said as we rode the elevator downstairs to the basement parking lot of the mall.

"We're friends Ariana and I'd like to be there for you," I said and smiled at her. "I'm still sure that I'm not your baby's dad but you mean a lot to me." That was the angle I'd decided to take.

I wasn't going to pretend to be the father of her baby but she needed a friend and I would be that friend. She didn't respond but I noticed that her eyes welled up. Good. I wanted guilt to eat at her. There was obviously another man who had had sex with her around the same time as I had and she'd figured I'd make the better father.

Either that or she genuinely believed I was the one who had gotten her pregnant.

"Thank you," she said when we reached her car. "I'll never forget this. Hope to see you soon."

"Of course," I said.

I let out a sigh of relief when she drove off. As soon as her car disappeared, she evaporated from my mind. I found my car and drove off, musing over what I was going to cook for dinner.

Very few people knew that side of me, and women less so. The only person who did was my ex-wife. When we were married, I used to be the one who did the cooking on the weekends when the chef was off. I'd probably taken after my dad, though his love had been baking.

By the time I parked in the grocery store parking, I'd already settled on a meal. Indian butter chicken and rice. Everyone loved chicken and Indian butter chicken was simple to make but delicious to eat.

I went into the store and bought the stuff I needed, including spices. Twenty minutes later, I was done and headed for home.

We'd agreed on six pm as the time when Maria would come over. I double checked my messages again to be sure that I'd pinned her my location. I had. I couldn't remember the last time I'd been this nervous and excited about having a woman come over to my place.

At twenty minutes to six, the food was ready and the wine chilling in the fridge. I'd already set the table and after one last inspection, I went to get ready.

I whistled as I showered, feeling stupidly happy. I took a deep breath and reminded myself that Maria and I were just lovers. Nothing more. No expectations and no secret hope that it could lead to something else.

What we had was insane chemistry and physical attraction. I'd seen women with prettier faces than Maria's and I'd met others with better figures, maybe, but I'd never met a woman who had the perfect package. Maria was the perfect package. The figure, the personality and the face.

I'd taken longer than I'd expected in the shower and I had to dress fast. Just as I finished buttoning my shirt, my house phone rang. I hurried to the night table to pick it up.

"Good evening sir," Adam, the lobby attendant said. "There's a lady by the name of Maria Swan here to see you."

"Evening Adam, let her in please," I said and replaced the receiver. My heart pounded hard as I went to the front door to let her in. I was excited like a fucking teenage boy.

What was the matter with me? Maria was just like any other woman. Even as I thought that, I knew that it wasn't true. She was different from the women I'd known in my past. For one, she was authentic. With Maria, what you saw was what you got.

She didn't pretend to be someone she wasn't and as someone who'd been surrounded by women falling over my feet when they learned my name, I appreciated that particular trait.

I stepped out my front door just as the elevator came to a stop. Maria stepped out and I found myself smiling widely like an idiot. Why did seeing her make me so fucking happy?

"Hi," she said softly in a voice that took me straight to bed.

My cock jerked in response. "Hello," I said and opened my arms.

She walked right into them and I held her tight, inhaling her sweet floral scent. Her body molded into mine as if we were made for each other. Wishful thinking, I chastised myself. That kind of thinking that would interfere with our perfect arrangement.

"Your home is beautiful," she said stepping out of my arms.

"Thanks," I said and led her through the front door. "Welcome."

"Thanks," she said.

I followed her in and stood beside her as she gazed around my apartment. "I didn't know that people lived like this," she exclaimed.

I was proud of my apartment. I'd spent a lot of time with the interior designer, getting it exactly how I wanted it. A private sanctuary where I could relax after work.

"I'm sure my interior designer still thinks I was a pain in the ass," I said.

"It's beautiful and so relaxing," she said. "You don't mind if I take off my shoes?" She stepped out of them before I could respond.

I laughed. It was going to be difficult to stop myself from having feelings for her. "Go on and make yourself at home."

She sat down on the couch and I excused myself to get the wine from the fridge. I was going to behave like a perfect gentleman and not give in to my longing which was to pull her into my arms, kiss her and then carry her to my bed.

I'd feed her first before having her for dessert.

I returned to the living room with the wine and glasses, and set them on the table.

"It feels so good to be here after the week I've had," she said.

I popped open the wine. "What happened? Everything okay at work?"

She shot me an amused look as I poured the wine. "Does your life revolve around work and nothing else?"

I beamed and handed her the glass of wine. "Pretty much."

"Well, mine doesn't," she said and paused to take a sip of her wine. She groaned after she'd swallowed it and naturally that reminded me of how she moaned in the throes of passion.

"This tastes like heaven," she said.

"I know something that tastes like heaven and it's not this wine," I flirted.

Her cheeks reddened. "I won't even ask what that is."

I joined her on the couch, making sure to sit far enough away that I wasn't tempted to grab her. "You were telling me about your week."

"Oh yes." She lifted her legs and tucked them under her body. "My sister Amber and her husband Jack have been trying to have a baby for the longest time. It's not working and IVF is super expensive so they asked me to surrogate for them."

I blinked rapidly as the meaning behind surrogacy sunk in. I'm a selfish bastard I'll admit and the first thing I thought was how that would affect our arrangement.

"What did you say?" I asked her.

"I haven't given them an answer yet but I think I'll say yes," she said. "Linda, that's my other sister, thinks that I'm an idiot."

I agreed with Linda but only for my selfish reasons.

"I know it's the right thing to do but honestly I wish it was any other time. I'm having such a good time right now. Business is picking and I'm so excited for the future," she said and then met my gaze and blushed.

I knew exactly what she was thinking. "I've never had sex with a pregnant woman. I think you'd be very sexy." I couldn't believe I had voiced my fucking sick thoughts.

She smiled. "Really? You'd have sex with me even when I'm pregnant?"

I nodded. "Nothing would keep me away."

"That's nice to know. It's inconveniencing and everything but I'd do anything for my sister. A baby would make her so happy."

It hit me then what a good person Maria is. She doesn't have a selfish bone in her body and here I was thinking of how the surrogacy would affect our relationship. I had no business messing with her. Maria was too good for me.

I hoped she had meant what she said about not wanting a relationship. She was the last person I'd ever want to hurt. Thinking such deep thoughts was making me restless and the plan had been to have a fun evening.

I drained the wine in my glass. "Ready for dinner?"

"Yes please, I'm starving," she said enthusiastically.

I stood and offered her my hand which she took. I should have dropped her hand when she stood up. Instead, I drew her up against me and she looped her arms around my neck.

My excuse was that her sexy floral scent intoxicated me and I couldn't think further than how lovely she smelled. I cupped her ass and pulled her closer to my erect cock. Her eyes rose in surprise before I sealed my mouth on hers and slipped my tongue into her mouth.

She moaned softly into my mouth and pressed her breasts against my chest. She was aroused too with her nipples taut and hard.

"You drive me crazy Maria," I whispered into her ear when we came up for air.

I caressed her face and searched her eyes. What was it about her that captivated me so much and made it impossible to have enough of her? Each time we had sex was better than the last one. The more layers I peeled off the more intrigued I became.

"I want to drive you crazy," she whispered back.

I captured her lower lip and gently bit on it. My hands fell to her soft shoulders before dropping to her breasts. I loved that she was wearing a blouse and a knee length skirt. I untucked her blouse and slipped my hands underneath to feel her skin.

"That feels so good," Maria said as I caressed her breasts.

"I love your breasts," I told her as I pulled down the cups of her bra. "Especially these." I thumbed her taut nipples and she let out sharp cries as though she was experiencing a mixture of pain and pleasure.

I tugged at them and then unable to resist, I lowered my head to suck on a nipple. As my mouth worked her nipples, I slipped a hand under her skirt and rubbed her pussy over her already damp panties. I hissed as I flicked my tongue over her nipples.

She was so fucking aroused. She had sit on my couch carrying on a conversation when all along she had been wanting me. Fuck. My cock swelled until I thought that it was going to explode.

MARIA

A loud rumble filled the air and I thought at first that it had come from Stephen until I saw the look of surprise on his face. Then he chuckled.

"I guess the way to a woman's heart is her stomach," he said as he pulled up my bra and rearranged my skirt.

"Did that come from me?" I said and when he nodded, I grinned. "I'm starving."

"Yeah, I figured that out. Go through that door to the kitchen, I'll be there in a bit," he said and disappeared down the hallway.

The kitchen was as gorgeous as the living room. Everything was stainless steel and pristine white. A beautiful large table sat in the middle of the room but what struck me was the lived-in feeling in the kitchen.

I'd not have been surprised to see a chef but there was no one. My stomach rumbled again at the delicious smells floating in the air.

"I'll just warm the stew," Stephen said coming into the kitchen.

"What are we having?" I said.

"Indian butter chicken and rice," he said.

"Sounds tasty. What do you want me to do?"

"It's ready and the table is set. Please have a seat," Stephen said.

I did as he asked and sat at one of the set places. It struck me how comfortable I had become with him. I saw him as a friend now but telling him about Amber and Jack's request had surprised me too. I was normally a private person when it came to personal matters.

Stephen brought the food to the table in serving dishes and then sat down on the other side of the table. "Let's dig in." He passed me the rice dish and then the chicken and salad.

"Your chef is a good cook," I said, idly wondering if he or she had left just before I got there.

Stephen burst out laughing. "I love how you say that in a matter-of-fact way. I don't have a chef or cook but I do have a cleaner who comes in every other day."

"So who cooked?" I said.

"Me," Stephen said.

I gaped at him. "You cook?"

"Yes. It surprises a lot of people. My father cooked too but he preferred to bake. I enjoy it. It relaxes me."

There was so much about him that surprised me and yes, it made me fall for him just a little bit more. I mean, what woman didn't love a man who could cook?

I took a first bite and moaned. "It's delicious. I need this recipe."

"I won't give you the recipe so that I'll always have an excuse to cook for you," Stephen said.

"Works for me," I said.

He cocked his head and contemplated me. "Tell me about your family."

I swallowed the food in my mouth. "There's not much to tell. We're your regular family. Parents, three girls. My older sister Amber is a hair stylist and married to Jack, a fire-fighter. As I told you, they don't have kids. Then there's Linda. She's a social worker and married to her job. My parents are retired but you wouldn't think so if you looked at their diaries."

I loved how soft and approachable Stephen looked when he smiled.

"What about you?" I said. "No siblings?"

"None. I asked for a brother for so many years until I got used to it. My mother later told me that they'd always wanted just one child."

"Yeah, she told me that," I said and immediately felt guilty as I hadn't returned her last phone call.

Sleeping with her son made it difficult to carry on the casual but nice friendship we'd enjoyed before.

"You two are pretty friendly I take it?" Stephen said.

"A little," I said. "Your mother is a wonderful woman."

"I was surprised when she offered you a franchise and yet you didn't meet all the conditions," Stephen said. "But after I met you, I understood why. You're captivating."

I laughed to dissolve the sudden intensity that had sprouted between us. "I don't think your mother thinks of me quite like that."

Stephen laughed. "No, that would be me."

All air left my lungs. Had he forgotten that we'd agreed to keep it light, in not so many words? "Thank you."

"I'm divorced though," Stephen said.

"Oh," I said, surprised by that piece of information. "What happened?"

He shrugged. "We wanted different things. For starters, she wanted a baby and I wasn't in a place in my life where I could be a good dad."

"Really? I think you'd make a wonderful dad," I said.

He shook his head. "Believe me, I wouldn't. I'm a workaholic, just like my father was. I wouldn't be there for my child and I'm glad Paige recognized that."

Just minutes ago, I'd felt so close to Stephen. So connected. Now he felt like a stranger. How could he talk about something so important like a baby and his belief in his inability to be a good father in such a detached manner? As if it didn't matter. "How can you say that?"

"Because it's the truth," he said. "Which reminds me, Paige is getting married this week and I'd like to go with you. It will be fun. There'll be good food for sure," he said. "Please."

"I hate weddings," I said Stephen was confusing me. Taking our relationship to the public implied that we were dating or becoming something more.

"I hate weddings too. We can bitch about it together," he said, making me laugh.

I made a snap decision. I was overthinking it and it was pretty simple. Stephen needed a woman on his arm to show his ex-wife that he had moved on. That was the only reason he had asked me to go with him. Not because there was anything more going on between us.

"Sure, why not?" I was also curious about the woman who had once been married to Stephen and one who had divorced him. I couldn't fathom anyone wanting to divorce him.

Besides being dynamite in the sack, he was great company and super intelligent. What more could a woman want?

"Tell me what's been happening at work?" he said, changing the topic abruptly.

I let out a sigh of relief. Work was a safe topic. "A lot I'd say. I contracted an IT specialist to do my website, something I've been pushing to the back burner for months. She'll have something for me to look at next week."

"Congratulations," Stephen said and sipped his water. "A website is important in this day and age."

I told him about the book I'd placed at the counter where my customers could sign up for our newsletter to hear about new products, discounts and other bakery related stuff. I planned to throw in nutritional stuff too as the Creamy Creations brand was big on healthy food.

They had a rigorous process for introducing a new product into their line but I looked forward to that challenge. For the first time in months, I was feeling excited for the future of my business.

"It's like a fire has been lit underneath your feet," Stephen said.

I grinned. "That's exactly how I feel." Since the conference, I'd come to view my business in a different way. I'd started to view it as a business and not just an outlet for my creativity.

It was fun too and not the chore I'd started to view it as. "Peter has also started working at the bakery full time," I said. It's eased a lot of my time and I can think of ways of growing the business."

Stephen nodded. "Don't be afraid to hire another baker, even if it'll be on a part-time basis. The time you spend away from the kitchen will be time spent marketing your business."

We talked business throughout dinner. He told me about his work as a venture capitalist. It sounded intriguing albeit frightening. The thought of investing hundreds of thousands of dollars into a startup frightened the daylights out of me.

Stephen laughed when I told him that. "It's not just startups. We also fund existing business that want to expand. Those make up about sixty percent of our business."

Time flew as we ate dinner, cleaned up and then carried our wine back to the living room. It was stimulating to talk shop with someone who understood the business so well.

Just as I drained the last of my wine, Stephen stood up. "I neglected to give you a tour of the apartment." He gave me his hand and I stood up.

"I'd love a tour." The last thing on my mind was a tour of the house. I had more urgent matters that needed attending to like the throb between my legs. Still I dutifully followed Stephen as he took me around the apartment which was at least three times the size of mine.

"I hope you brought your nightgown," Stephen said when I entered the master bedroom. "I intend to keep you captive here overnight."

It was spacious and beautiful. The kind of room you would happily lock yourself in for months at a time and never leave. "I love it," I said and threw myself on the bed and rolled onto my back.

"You look beautiful Maria," Stephen said, staring down at me. "I couldn't resist even if I wanted to."

He climbed on after me and draped his body over mine and looked into my face. "So, did you bring your night gown?"

"I sleep naked," I said.

His eyes widened. "A woman after my own heart." He lowered his head and kissed me gently on the lips. "I've thought about you all day."

My heart pounded crazily in my chest. "Me too," I admitted. Not just that day. I thought about him all the time. He was never far off from my mind and it frightened me.

I'd never had a relationship that was just physical. I didn't know the rules. Was I breaking them by fantasizing about a future with him? Was I going down a road that would lead to heartbreak? Was he feeling it too or were the words leaving his mouth just sweet talk?

All thought left my mind as Stephen cradled my face and deepened the kiss. Our tongues met in a wet, hot slide. He pressed his hardness against me and I raised my hips, aching to feel all of him. I slid my hands over his back to cup his perfect hard ass.

Stephen moved from my mouth and trailed kisses down my neck and slid down to my breasts. He pushed my blouse up, and buried his head in the valley between my breasts.

"You smell edible," he said and I giggled.

"You too." He smelled of his signature cologne and freshness.

I reached down and popped open the top buttons of my blouse and then pulled it over my head. Stephen kissed the tops of my breasts and my nipples strained against the material of my bra.

"So perfect," he said as my chest rose up and down.

I raked my fingers through my hair and fought down my longing to have his hands on me. He nuzzled my breasts, licking and sucking over my bra until I couldn't take it anymore.

"Let's get the bra off," I said.

Stephen chuckled. "I was waiting to see how long you would last. Not long."

"Not with you, no," I said as Stephen reached behind me and expertly unclasped my bra.

He must have done it countless times. The thought crossed my mind before I could check it and a burning sensation in my chest followed it. Jealousy. I hated myself for it. Of course, Stephen had been with other women just as I'd been with other men.

In addition to that, we had no claim on each other. I had no right to feel jealous or possessive.

Then his mouth was on my hard nipples and thoughts of other women left my mind and it was just me and him. I arched my back and let out a long moan of satisfaction and pleasure.

My nipples were more sensitive than they normally were and I felt as if I would come just from Stephen's mouth on them. It was torturous pain when Stephen flicked them with his tongue and then bit them gently.

"That feels so good," I said.

He moved lower and when he got to my skirt, he pulled it down and I wiggled out of it, leaving me with just my panties. Stephen spread my legs and slid lower until his head was between my legs. How did I get so lucky to land a man who loved giving pleasure, more than he enjoyed receiving it?

"Oh God," I cried as he teased my clit with the tip of his tongue, driving me to a near climax.

"Give me a sec," he said in a deep growl.

I followed him with hooded eyes as he stood by the side of the bed and peeled off his clothes. His thick, long cock stood at attention and the thought of it inside me made my thighs tremble. I wanted to feel every contour of his cock. I got on all fours.

"You look so hot from this angle," Stephen said as he got behind me. "Spread your legs for me."

I did and we both moaned as he slid his cock up and down the folds of my pussy. It felt like an eternity when he finally pushed his cock inside me, and rammed into me until my body melted into his with a toe-curling orgasm.

MARIA

I turned the bakery key at half passed four in the morning. I loved this hour of the morning when the city was quiet. I was a morning person and found it calming when it was my turn to open the bakery. Peter did most early mornings though as it worked well for him to get to work early and leave early.

I flicked the lights on as I entered through the back delivery door. I inhaled the scent of cake and bread that lingered in the air and my lips pulled into a smile. If there was one thing I never doubted in my life, it was my career. Baking was what I wanted to do for the rest of my life.

I made my first cup of coffee and sat down to drink it before the deliveries started to arrive. I brought the cup to my mouth, inhaling the aroma of the coffee before it hit my mouth. I took the first sip and as soon as I swallowed it, I gagged on it. I quickly rose, went to the trash can and spit the coffee out.

After that, I couldn't make myself drink it. I made tea instead and to my surprise, it went down well, unlike the coffee.

The deliveries started arriving and I spent the next fifteen minutes checking them against what we had ordered the previous day.

When that was done, I cleaned up and started on breads, rolls, cakes and muffins. As I worked, I made plans for the day. The first thing I needed to do was to call Amber. I'd procrastinated telling her my decision for too long and it wasn't fair. I knew the reason for it.

My telling her would mark the beginning of the end between Stephen and me. Sure, he'd said that he would find me sexy when I was pregnant, but I was sure that was just talk. The reality was bound to be a lot different. I just didn't see Stephen hanging around a pregnant woman.

The delay hadn't been in vain either. I'd used that time to do some research on pregnancy especially. I'd read that a lot of women were able to work throughout their pregnancies as long as it was a normal pregnancy.

I was physically strong and I was sure that I was in that group of women who worked until the last weeks. Now that I had Peter, I was feeling confident that I could do it without it negatively affecting my business.

The rest of the guys started coming in at six and by then I already had the first batch in the oven. Mornings were busy as we got ready for our early morning customers who came in to get their breakfast.

Nine AM found me in my office with my second cup of tea, reading and responding to my emails. Our custom orders had increased ten-fold which meant that a lot of my time was spent corresponding with those customers.

I took a break from my computer and grabbed my phone to call Amber. She started her work day a little later as they stayed well past seven at the beauty salon. She answered her phone on the first ring as though she had been sitting staring at it.

"Hello sister," she said, her voice tinged with worry.

Sympathy for her flooded me. I couldn't imagine how it felt to want something so bad and yet you can't make it happen. My sister had always been very independent. She'd started working in beauty salons at a young age and she was the kid who started earning at a young age.

It must have been very difficult for her to ask for help. Thinking about it made me glad that I'd decided to help her. "Hey Amber."

"What's up?" she said.

I swallowed hard. The moment the words were out of my mouth, I knew that I had committed to going ahead with the surrogacy arrangement.

"I've made a decision," I said. "I'm going to do it. I'm going to carry the baby for you and Jack."

There was silence from the other end of the phone. Then came the sound of muffled crying. Then I was also crying.

"I don't know what to say. I love you. I love you. I love you. Jack is going to be so excited when I tell him. We're going to have a baby," Amber said.

I laughed. "Not too fast. We have to get me pregnant first."

"I know, I know," she said. "This is so exciting. Thank you so much Maria. There are no words to say how much this means to me. Thank you."

"It's okay."

"Now, let's get down to business," Amber said.

"Business?" I said.

"I already spoke to the people at the clinic and they are ready for you."

That took me a back and I was silent for a while as I digested it. Before I could say anything, she continued to talking.

"There are some tests you need to get done and they have several counseling sessions before the procedure is done."

"Wow hang on," I said. "Why would you make those arrangements without knowing whether I would agree?"

Amber laughed sheepishly. "I had a feeling you would. You're my sister. I know you."

That pissed me off. I told myself to stop being petty. "What if I said no?" I asked her unable to let it go.

"That would be Linda. You don't have it in you to say no," Amber said in a dismissive tone.

She was implying that I was a doormat which I wasn't. Just because I'd have done anything for my sisters did not make me a doormat.

"Anyway, I'll tell them that you'll be there tomorrow."

Her attitude was seriously annoying me. I got that she was excited about the baby but she was taking me for granted. It would have been nice if she had asked about my schedule before committing me to the clinic.

I let out a sigh. "Fine, what time?"

"I'll message you and give you all the information you need. Do you want me there with you tomorrow?"

"I'll be fine," I said in crisp tones.

When we ended the call, it left me with a bad taste in my mouth. Instead of feeling happy that I was doing something selfless for my sister, I felt used and unappreciated.

We all knew Amber could be selfish but I reminded myself that this was something she wanted really badly. Her behavior was understandable.

Linda passed by the bakery as I was in the process of closing. She entered the kitchen darting her eyes around like a thief. "Lover boy in here?"

I laughed. "Why would Stephen be hiding? He's got nothing to hide."

He'd texted me that morning and every morning since the night I spent at his apartment. Short sweet messages wishing me a productive day. No one could accuse Stephen of not being romantic but I liked it. I'd gone out with romantic guys and none of them had come close to making me feel as special as Stephen did.

"Coffee?" Linda asked, turning on the coffee machine.

"No thanks," I said. "For some reason, it's not agreeing with me now. I'll have tea instead."

"I called Amber this morning," I told Linda when we settled down with our hot drinks.

"You told her you'd do it?" Linda said.

I nodded and then narrated for her the whole conversation.

"Amber has always been selfish," Linda said quietly. "I'll come with you to the clinic. You shouldn't be alone."

"What about work?"

"Don't worry about that. I'll figure something out."

It was on the tip of my tongue to protest when it dawned on me that I did want someone there with me. Someone to reassure me that I was doing the right thing.

"Yes, please and I would love it if you'd pretend that you think it's a good idea," I said. "I need your support Sis."

"You have it," Linda said. "How come you're not meeting lover boy tonight?"

"Who said I'm not?" I threw back and then laughed at her expression. "I'm seeing him on Saturday. We're going to his ex-wife's wedding."

Linda's eyes widened. "They are civilized, aren't they?"

I giggled. "They are. I'm not sure I'd attend my ex-husband's wedding. I would make sure I was out of town. I have to say though, I'm curious to meet the woman who divorced Stephen."

"She was the one who divorced him?" Linda asked.

I nodded.

"Something is seriously wrong with your lover boy," she said. "No one divorces a billionaire."

I laughed. "Oh I know why she divorced him. She wanted children and she didn't think Stephen had what it takes to be a good dad."

"Interesting," was all Linda said. "Anyway, you've inspired me to go out more. There's this guy who owns the salad bistro I frequent. He asked me out and I said yes."

I beamed. "Linda, that's great! Good for you. I'm glad you get to have some fun."

We sat around chatting and when it was time to leave, I hugged her tight, feeling overly emotional in a way I'd never felt before.

"Thanks for offering to go with me," I said, fighting back sudden tears.

The whole business was turning me into an emotional mess. If I was like that before I even became pregnant, my hormones would go haywire when I had an actual baby in my belly.

STEPHEN

Shopping for baby clothes was fine and so was receiving texts from Ariana fifty times a day because I could ignore them. But asking me to go for breakfast with her first thing when I got to the office was too much. I remembered Jeremy's advice and wrote her back saying I'd meet her in an hour.

Resentment bubbled inside my throat. It was fucking annoying to have to tip toe around a woman who was carrying another man's child. I grabbed my phone and asked my secretary to bring me strong, black coffee. Then I turned on my computer, hoping to lose myself in my emails for the next hour.

Maria's beautiful face popped into my brain and my irritation went down a notch. She was probably at work now. I'd fallen into a habit of texting her every morning and I reached for my phone.

Me: Good morning. How was your night?

I was surprised when she texted me back immediately. Usually it took her a couple of hours to respond to messages, which I understood. Her mornings were busy in the bakery kitchen.

Maria: Morning! I had a good night. Hope you did too.

Me: I did, thanks. At the office now but will pop out for a bit to meet someone. What are your plans for the day?

Maria: I'm going to the clinic to get some preliminary tests done. Not looking forward to that. I'm scared of needles.

Me: I'll come and hold your hand.

Maria: Really?

Me: Really.

Maria: Thanks!

The irony did not escape me. Here I was offering to take Maria to a clinic where she was going to get artificially inseminated with another couple's sperm and egg, while I was resentful of meeting a pregnant woman for coffee.

Well, I liked one a little bit too much, while I barely tolerated the other. By the time my secretary brought the coffee, I was in a much better mood. The prospect of seeing Maria changed my day from dull to exciting.

An hour later, I left and took a walk down the block to the Starbucks where I was meeting Ariana. I'd made sure to leave a few minutes late so that she would be there when I arrived. She was seated in a corner sipping on her coffee.

"You took too long and I got my coffee," she said.

"That's fine," I said and stared at her expectantly. I wanted to make it clear that it was not a date.

My working hours were precious and I was not going to entertain having them wasted.

"Aren't you going to get your coffee?" she said.

"No, I'm fine." I glanced at my watch. "I have a meeting back in the office in a few minutes."

"Fine, I get the message," Ariana said and set her cup back on the table. "I'll get straight to why I wanted to see you. I'm sure this will be good news for you. After doing some calculations with my doctor, we think you might not be the father of my baby after all."

I met her gaze. "I know."

She blinked rapidly. "You know?"

"I wore a condom and I did not ejaculate that night," I said.

She bit her lip and then raked a hand through her hair. "Oh. Anyway, you're off the hook."

I had so much I wanted to say, all of which ended or begun with an expletive. I inhaled deeply and told myself she was pregnant.

"The father is—" she started to say but I raised my hand to stop her.

"I'm not interested in knowing who I was sharing your bed with," I said.

"That's not fair! He's my boyfriend and he was there before I met you," she said hotly.

"Then why did you say that I was the father?" I said, my control slipping.

"What are you complaining about?" Ariana said. "My boyfriend has taken responsibility for the baby and I'm not suing you for millions. Everyone wins."

Disgust filled me. It was one thing to suspect that Ariana had wanted to pin her pregnancy on me for the money but to have it confirmed, sickened me.

"Take care of yourself," I said and stood up.

"I will," she said cheerfully as if she had not wasted several weeks of my precious time.

I glanced at my watch. There was no time to go back to the office. I'd promised Maria that I'd be at the clinic at noon. I flagged down a cab and gave him the address of the clinic. I texted Jeremy and let him know that we could exhale now. Ariana had admitted that I wasn't the father of her baby.

I was glad that I'd found Maria. She was honest and believed in hard work to get what she wanted. I was safe from predatory women for now and I could let loose and have fun with Maria. It didn't bother me that soon she was going to be pregnant. I found women's bodies beautiful in whatever size or shape.

The cab came to a stop in front of the clinic and I paid the driver and stepped out. I hurried in and when I entered the reception room, I saw Maria. Her face lit up in a smile when she saw me.

"Hi," she said and stood up. She threw her hands around me in a hug which made me feel warm all over.

I held her close. "Hello."

"Thanks for coming," she said, tugging at my hand to sit down with her. "It's a good thing you offered. Linda was supposed to be here too but something urgent came up at work."

"That's the social worker?" I said.

"Yes," Maria said. She narrowed her eyes as she looked at me. "It's too early to look tired."

I sighed. "I'm not tired. I'm relieved and upset at the same time."

"Those two words don't belong in the same sentence."

I laughed, all the tension in my body evaporating. "They shouldn't but when I tell you what happened, you'll understand." I surprised myself by telling her the whole sorry tale.

"The baby could still be yours," Maria said.

"No it's not. I wore a condom that night and before you tell me that they tear, trust me it didn't and I didn't ejaculate." I'd said it so many times that it had ceased to feel like a private matter.

Maria's eyes widened. "So why do you think she picked you?"

I shrugged. "Same reason women do. The money."

Maria was silent for a moment. "That's a horrible way to live being suspicious about people's motivations."

"A baby practically guarantees that she won't ever lack all her life," I said.

"Is that what you really believe about women?" she said quietly.

"Tell me this. Why would a woman get pregnant with a man she barely knows and without having that conversation with him?"

"Maybe you're right."

"It sucks to know that most women are only interested in you because of your bank balance but when you find a woman who is genuine, it's a real pleasure," I said and held her gaze.

Her cheeks reddened but before she could say anything, the receptionist called her name.

"I'll be here," I said. While I was happy to hold her hand before and after, I had no desire to witness them poking and prodding Maria.

"I'll see you soon," she said.

I watched her as she walked away, swaying her hips slightly. God she was beautiful and I didn't know how the hell I was going to stay away when our arrangement came to an end.

I kept myself occupied by reading and responding to emails on my phone. Maria was gone for an hour but it went by fast.

"I'm sorry it took so long," she said when she returned to the waiting area. "They took a sample of everything apart from my brain." She made a face.

I stood up. "It's fine. I've managed to empty my inbox and that's a feat in itself." I studied her face. "You look tired."

"I do feel tired," she said.

"Let's get you home then," I said. "You don't need to be at the bakery, do you?"

"No, I got all the morning baking done and Peter is closing up today," Maria said.

I mentally rearranged my schedule. I had nothing pressing scheduled in the afternoon. "I'll cook us some lunch while you relax."

She glanced at me from head to toe. "You're dressed for it too."

I laughed and patted the jacket of my suit. "When this comes off and I roll up the sleeves of my shirt, it'll be go time."

We joked and teased as we left the clinic. We took a cab to her place and used the back door to access her apartment.

"Are you ashamed of me?" I teased her as I followed her up the stairs.

I couldn't see her face but I was sure that her cheeks had turned pinked.

"Of course not but my private life is private," she said.

"So you are ashamed of me," I said lightly.

When we entered her apartment, Maria shut the door and faced me. "I don't know how long this will last and like you said, it's all fun and games. Why would I want my employees knowing about us and then asking me later where you disappeared to? Does that make sense?"

My chest constricted painfully at the reminder that what we had would end. But she was right. We were not planning a future together and the less people who knew about us, the better.

"I was teasing." I cupped her face and brushed my lips against hers. "Now put up your feet on the couch and rest. I'll see what you have in the fridge and get started with lunch."

Maria sighed. "That sounds like heaven."

I laughed. She dropped her purse on the table, kicked off her shoes and got comfortable on the couch. I arranged a light throw over her legs.

"Thank you," she said. "I don't know why I feel so beat."

"Probably a lot of emotional stuff going on," I said. "It can't be easy deciding to carry a baby for your sister."

Maria sniffed. "It's not. When I told her that I would yesterday, she told me that the clinic people were ready for me."

I stared at her blankly and then understanding dawned. I frowned. "She was that sure you were going to say yes?"

Maria nodded miserably. "She launched into our plans for the next few weeks, all without asking me whether it was okay with me."

Her sister was a selfish bitch but I wasn't going to say that aloud. At the end of the day, she was still her sister. "I'm sure that she didn't mean to be like that. People do crazy things when they're over-excited."

Maria's face lost the pinched look. "I guess you're right."

I kissed her forehead and then shrugged out of my jacket and flung it on the arm rest. "I'll be in the kitchen."

If my team saw me now, they would think I'd gone insane, I

mused as I flung Maria's fridge open and sifted through the contents. Minutes later, I'd decided what to make for lunch. Beef and mushrooms with mashed potatoes.

I washed my hands and gathered the ingredients, placing them on the counter. In another life I could have been a chef rather than a venture capitalist. Cooking would have given me the same sense of satisfaction as my investment projects did.

Soon delicious smells filled the kitchen. I enjoyed cooking for Maria. It hit me then that it wasn't just cooking for her that I enjoyed. I loved taking care of her as well. Take that afternoon for instance. It had brought me joy to be there for her at the clinic.

That was sobering and frightening. It meant that I was developing feelings for her. What would happen when she decided that she wanted us to stop sleeping together? Pregnancy affected women differently. By opening my heart to her, I was setting myself up for disappointment and pain.

The trouble was that it was too late. I liked her a little too much. What man wouldn't though? She was sexy and beautiful and smart.

MARIA

The first thing I noticed when I woke up was that it was night time and Stephen was still in my apartment. He was seated with his legs propped up on the table, his face cutely screwed up in concentration. The last thing I remembered was closing my eyes just for a few minutes while I waited for lunch to be ready.

It seemed as though I had slept all afternoon. I must have been more exhausted than I thought. I couldn't remember the last time I had slept during the day. My stomach rumbled, breaking the silence.

"You're awake," Stephen said, swinging his gaze to me.

"Good evening," I said. "I can't believe I slept all afternoon. What time is it?"

He beamed. "Seven."

I swung my legs to the ground and sat up. "Did you go back to work?"

"No, I sent someone to bring my laptop," Stephen said.

"I'm sorry for ruining your work day," I said, guilt flooding me. I knew how busy Stephen was at work. In essence, he was overseeing two businesses. His own Investment company and Creamy Creations.

"You didn't ruin my day, on the contrary. I haven't felt this relaxed in a long time," he said. "The only thing I felt bad about is that you didn't eat. I'll warm you a plate."

"You don't have to," I said and yawned. "I can do it."

"I insist," he said.

I should have been feeling rested after all that sleep but what I felt like doing was curling my feet up and falling asleep again. Weird. I told this to Stephen when he returned with my dinner tray.

"You're probably coming down with something. Finish eating and go to bed. We want you fresh for tomorrow," he said.

It felt like heavy stones were sitting on my eyelids. I could barely keep them open. I managed to finish the delicious beef, mushrooms and potatoes.

"Let's get you to bed," Stephen said.

He went as far as helping me change out of my clothes into a nightgown.

"I'll stay with you until you fall asleep then I'll let myself out," he said.

"I'm such a useless host," I said, in between yawns.

Stephen chuckled. "It's just today and it's understandable. You'll be back to yourself tomorrow." He kissed my forehead.

~

I woke up startled as I found myself in total darkness. My last memory was of Stephen stroking my hair and whispering sweet nothings into my ear. I blinked several times until my eyes got used to the darkness. I rolled onto my side to look at my night clock.

Three twenty-five in the morning. Five minutes before my wake-up time. I felt energetic and fresh. The wedding was in the afternoon and I'd planned take the morning shift. I sat up in bed, glad that the fatigue that had been with me all day yesterday was gone. All I'd needed was a mega nap to feel like myself again.

Stephen had been right. I did feel like a new person. I reached under the pillow for my phone. I smiled when I saw the message from him.

Stephen: I bet you woke up in the middle of the night in a panic. Take a deep breath in. All is well. I hope you're feeling great and I'll see you tomorrow morning.

I contemplated texting him back then thought otherwise. It wouldn't be fair to wake him up and he was probably a light sleeper. I slipped out of bed and padded into the bathroom to get ready for the day.

Lucky for me, I wasn't a high maintenance person and in fifteen minutes, I was downstairs opening the back door of the bakery. I felt like a new person as I went through my morning routine.

Keziah came in at six and the others slowly trickled in. Beth was usually the last to arrive just before half passed seven. She was a single mom and usually had to drop her toddler son off at her mother's, who took care of him when she was at work.

"Hey you," Beth said popping into the office where I'd gone to update our orders that went out later in the day.

"Hi," I said, looking up from my screen.

"My you look chirpy this morning," she said.

"I feel chirpy. Would you believe that after the clinic appointment, I went home and slept until this morning?"

"Fatigue probably," Beth said. "It's a state I'm pretty familiar with but it's better now that Luke is three years old."

"I don't know how you did it alone," I said.

Luke's dad had left her when he found out that she was pregnant and she had raised him alone since then.

"How did it go at the clinic?" Beth said, her tone sympathetic.

Other than Stephen, she was the only one I'd told about my decision to surrogate for my sister. "Loads of tests but thank God that part's over."

"Did you have someone with you?" she said.

She knew that Stephen and I had developed a good professional relationship. "Yeah, I did. Stephen went with me."

Beth raised an eyebrow. "Me thinks you two are warming each other's beds."

I laughed. "Maybe."

"If you are, I'm happy for you. You deserve all the happiness Maria."

"Thanks. As a matter of fact, we're going to a wedding together this afternoon."

Beth's gazed moved to my hair. "Really? Are you planning on doing something about that hair? And maybe those nails?"

I threaded my fingers through my hair. "Sure, I'll give it a wash."

Beth rolled her eyes. "You're hopeless. Do something special today. You only need two hours with my hair dresser and you'll come out looking like a movie star. I'll call her and make an emergency appointment for you."

When I wanted to get my hair professionally done, I usually went to the beauty salon where my sister worked. It wouldn't do now as it would invite a lot of questions from Amber. Not to mention that I was also still mad at her.

"Beth—"

She moved to the door. "No excuses. Treat yourself."

I was still smiling when she shut the door behind her. I wasn't averse to looking like a movie star for the day. She returned five minutes later to tell me that I had an appointment at eleven.

After thanking her, I shut the computer and got a move on. I still had a lot to do in the kitchen before Peter came in for his shift.

The morning flew by and at half past ten, Beth came and shooed me out of the bakery with instructions to enjoy the day and night to the fullest. Pinpricks of excitement lit up my skin at the thought of spending the afternoon in Stephen's company. It had been a long time since I'd had a fun evening out and I was looking forward to it.

I gave the cab driver the beauty salon address and when I got there, I found that Carol, the hair stylist was waiting for me. It was nice to lie back and enjoy a bit of pampering. Carol trimmed and did other magical things to my hair and an hour later, I really did resemble a movie star.

I couldn't wait to get into the dress I'd picked for the wedding. Even though I was low maintenance, my secret vice was clothes. I loved dresses even though I rarely got an opportunity to dress up.

When I got to my apartment, I showered and returned to spruce myself up. I slathered myself in a perfumed body lotion, put on a little mascara and lip gloss and finally wore the beige, knee length, cocktail dress I'd picked.

I stared at my reflection in the mirror and liked what I saw. I was glad that I'd let Beth talk me into getting my hair done. There was nothing like a visit to the beauty salon to leave you feeling like a million dollars.

I needed it too since I was going to finally meet Stephen's ex-wife. Stephen rang the bell at half passed one and rather than let him up, I grabbed my purse and headed down the stairs.

"You look stunning," Stephen said, his gaze rippling up and down my body.

"Thanks. You look pretty hot yourself," I said, admiring the figure he cut in a black jacket and a crisp white shirt.

"Thank you," he said. "This way."

He led me to a limo parked on the side of the street and opened the back door for me. He followed me in and introduced me to his driver. When we started moving, he pressed a button and a glass partition rose up, separating us from the driver.

"This is nice," I said, looking around the spacious interior.

Stephen inched closer until he was right next to me. He slid a hand along my jaw and then leaned in to kiss me. I sighed and parted my lips to draw him in.

"I've been thinking of doing this all day," he murmured and then kissed me again.

My body awoke as if it had been in deep slumber and shots of desire stole over me. The kiss was long and leisurely and I moaned softly as the passion between us grew from a smoldering fire to a full burn.

Stephen groaned and moved away, then gestured at the tent in front of his pants. "If we don't stop now, I'll be a walking embarrassment. No other woman has ever turned me on as much as you do."

His words should have made me feel good, desirable and sexy. They didn't. What they did was remind me that what we had was merely physical. I was about to meet the type of woman who got Stephen to put a ring on it and not just share his bed.

He leaned back in the chair. "I'm glad the exhaustion is gone," he said, continuing with the communication we had been having via text message.

"I woke up feeling brand new," I said. "Thank you for making me dinner last night. It was delicious."

"She says a day later," Stephen teased. He took a strand of my hair and toyed with it. "Your hair is so soft. Everything about you is soft and womanly."

I grew more curious about Paige. I couldn't wait to see her. "I hope that's a good thing."

"It's the best thing. Women should be soft and curvy," he said, his words rolling over me like a caress.

My body heated up all over again. Stephen was the only man I'd ever met who could get me hot with just words. He placed his hand on my bare knee and softly massaged it. He made tiny circles that widened dangerously until his fingers were grazing my panties.

My breath quickened and my chest rose up. "What are you doing?" I said. "My panties are going to soak right through," I whispered.

"Can I feel how wet you are?" he said.

I brought my legs together. "No. That will make it worse."

"Please," Stephen said.

I would do anything for him if he pleaded. I parted my thighs and he dipped his hand between my thighs. He ran a finger over my pussy and I let out a desperate hungry sound.

"Oh God." I knew it was a mistake letting him touch me there. I wanted more.

He slipped a finger under the hem of my panties and I spread my legs further inviting him to do more. With deft fingers, he found my clit and rubbed circles around it, increasing the speed and pressure after every few seconds.

"Please," I pleaded. I couldn't believe how close I was to coming, just from a mere touch and rub.

He rubbed me faster. I gripped his hand as if hanging on it for dear life. Then my body exploded and I came on his hand.

MARIA

It was a beautiful setting for a garden wedding. The theme colors were gorgeous, purple and white, with an arch at the front made from purple and white flowers. Stephen and I got there on time and as soon as we sat down, it was time for the ceremony to begin.

"Did you have a big wedding?" I whispered to Stephen.

He grinned and shook his head. "We eloped to Vegas. My mother never forgave me for that," he said and I giggled. "It was an impromptu decision and clearly a wrong one."

The music came on and it was time for the wedding to start. The groom and his groomsmen lined up at the front. I mused over how Stephen must be feeling about to witness his ex-wife say her vows to another man.

The bridesmaids walked down the aisle dancing and then the first bars of the wedding march came on and we all stood. My first glimpse of Paige had me gasp but then so did everyone else. Paige was beautiful. Her blond hair was held up in a fancy hairdo at the tip of her head and she had a heart shaped face that was perfect.

Confidence oozed out of her as she walked down the aisle holding on to a man I assumed to be her father. Her stomach was nicely rounded and protruding the slightest bit. She was definitely pregnant. When she went by our pew, she looked towards Stephen and smiled.

The groom's face radiated the love he had for his bride. Whatever other reasons Paige might had had for getting married, the one thing she had gotten right was the love part. The bride and groom had no eyes for anyone else as the ceremony commenced.

It was a beautiful ceremony and when they exchanged their own hand written vows, I had tears in my eyes. I wished I could see Stephen's face but I had a feeling that he was just fine. There was a detachment about him when he spoke about his ex-wife.

As if he had moved on.

After the ceremony, we moved a few steps to the hotel ballroom where the reception was being held. "That was so touching," I said to Stephen as we sat down at our table.

"It was. I hope that Paige will finally be happy," he said cheerfully.

The food like everything else about the wedding, was delicious. Later, after the bride and groom had had their first dance, Stephen took me to the dance floor for a slow one. It was nice being out in public with him and being ourselves.

Later in the evening, Paige and her new husband did the rounds of the room, saying hello to everyone. She made it to our table by herself and Stephen and I stood up.

I watched as they hugged and was proud of myself that the pang I'd felt earlier was gone. She was clearly in love with her new husband and as for Stephen, he might as well have been attending a friend's wedding for all the emotion he showed.

"Thank you so much for coming. It means a lot to me," Paige said to Stephen.

"I couldn't miss it," Stephen said and then took my hand. "This is my date, Maria Swan."

Paige flashed me a genuine smile. "It's a pleasure to meet you. I hope you're having a great time."

"It's nice to meet you too," I said. "I'm enjoying myself, thank you and congratulations."

She joined her husband after that and Stephen and I danced to one more song, before he whispered into my ear that we should leave. The limo was waiting outside and the driver opened the passenger door when he saw us.

"Thank you for coming with me. It was unexpectedly fun," Stephen said.

"You're welcome. Paige is lovely," I said.

"She's a good person. We were just wrong for each other," he said. "We should have remained friends. We had so little in common."

Stephen's phone rang and he reached for it in the pocket of his jacket. It was a business call and as he spoke, I took the opportunity to turn on my phone. It flashed with multiple messages and calls.

All the calls were from Linda and Amber. My heart pounded hard in my chest. I called Amber back.

"Hey," she said. "I've been trying to get hold of you."

"What's up?" I said.

"The clinic called me. We're at mom and dads. Can you pass by?" she said.

"Is everything okay?" I said.

"Everything's fine. Just come, will you?"

"Okay." I was a bit miffed that my plans were changing. When we were dancing together, Stephen had whispered to me the things he planned to do to me when we got home.

"Change of plans," I told Stephen when I disconnected the call. "Amber and Linda are at my parents and they asked me to meet them there."

"Okay, sure," he said and told the driver that our plans had changed. I gave him my parents' address.

"Can you come to my place after you're done?" Stephen said.

"Nothing can keep me away," I said.

He leaned forward and kissed me softly and lightly on my mouth. I tried to figure out why Amber would call me unexpectedly to my parents' house and why the clinic had called her and not me. Maybe they had tried to call me but had found my phone switched off.

When we neared my parents' home, I grabbed the silky shawl I had left in the passenger seat and arranged it around my shoulders.

"Do you want us to wait for you?" Stephen said.

"No, I'll be fine. One of my sisters will drop me off," I said, my body muscles tight with tension.

The limo came to a stop and after kissing Stephen, I opened the door and got out. The driver didn't move until the front door swung open.

"You look beautiful," my mom said as she let me in.

I kissed her cheek and strolled in. "Thank you. I was at a wedding."

"Oh, how nice. A friend of yours?" she said.

"A friend of a friend's," I said.

Dad, Linda and Amber were in the living room. I kissed each of them and shot a questioning look at Linda. She shrugged. Clearly no one else knew why Amber had called us.

We made chit chat as I told them about the wedding but I was growing impatient. I was tired and I wanted to be with Stephen at that moment.

"What's going on?" I asked Amber.

"As I told you, I got a call from the clinic and I thought I should let everyone know at the same time what they told me."

I couldn't read the expression on Amber's face. Muted shock. Anger. I wasn't sure which one it was but she was definitely not herself.

"What did they say?" Mom asked.

Amber met my gaze. "They said you tested positive for pregnancy."

Her words did not immediately make sense.

"But she hasn't gotten the procedure done yet," Linda said.

Amber's eyes were cold and hard as she stared at me. I was pregnant! Everything fell into place then. The nausea I'd been feeling when I drank coffee. The extreme fatigue.

"Oh my God," I finally said as it dawned on me that I was carrying a real live human in my body.

"I thought you said you were not seeing someone," Amber said, barely containing her anger.

"I'm not. We're not serious," I stammered.

Stephen. I'd not considered him in all that. I was pregnant with his baby. His words came to me as if he was right there saying them again.

Why would a woman get pregnant with a man she barely knows and without having that conversation with him?

I had agreed with him. Little had I known that I was that woman he was talking about. Dismay came over me. He would think that I had plotted to get pregnant too so as to get his money. Nausea rose up my throat.

"Maria!" my mother said sharply. "You're not serious and yet you're sleeping with him?"

I brought my attention back to the present. I felt like a teenager again. For all of a minute and then I squared my shoulders. "Look, I'm sorry that I've ruined all our plans but the fact is I'm pregnant and an adult and I can take care of my child."

"It's not about you, you selfish—" Amber burst out crying. "We wanted this so badly and now you've ruined it."

"I'm sorry," I said and unconsciously placed a hand on my belly.

"Maybe something can come of this," Mother said. "Do you want a baby?" she said to me.

I stared at her in confusion. "What do you mean? Do I have a choice? I'm already pregnant."

"Yes you do. You're single and not in a stable relationship and you're also busy with your work. Why not go ahead with the arrangement and assume that the baby is Amber's. Let her adopt your baby."

Silence fell in the room.

"That is messed up," Linda said. "It's the sickest thing I've ever heard. Listen Mom, I know you want Amber to have her baby, we all do but this stops here. Amber and Jack will save up like other couple's do and get IVF. We'll all chip in too where we can."

I could have hugged Linda. We all knew that Amber was my mother's favorite child and it didn't bother us in any way but asking me to give my baby to her? Like Linda had said, that was sick.

My dad sat staring at us as if he was wondering how in God's name, we were related to him. I didn't blame him. This whole business was becoming a bad soap opera.

"Why don't you let Maria decide for herself," Amber said, staring at me hard.

I held her gaze. "I really wanted to do this for you and Jack but Amber, you don't just give a baby away."

"You were going to," she said.

"Yes, but this one's mine and Stephen's, not yours and Jack's. Stephen has a right to know that he's going to be a father."

She slumped back into her seat and tears welled up in her eyes.

"I'm sorry." I felt horrible for disappointing her but as the shock wore off, I became secretly pleased that I was pregnant with my own baby.

As ready as I had been to surrogate for my sister, I'd been coerced into the idea. My motivation had been guilt and a sense of responsibility towards my sister's happiness.

I needed to leave and get away from Mom and Amber's accusing stares. I shot to my feet. "I have to go. I'll talk to you soon."

Linda stood up too. "I'll drive you home."

No one said anything as Linda and I walked out.

"That's the weirdest evening I've ever had," she said when we got into her car. She took my hand and smiled. "You're going to have a baby! I'm going to be an aunty."

I smiled as tension left my body. "I know. It's exciting."

"It is. What do you think Stephen's reaction will be?" Linda said.

I shifted my glance to her. "I don't think I'll tell him."

Linda's jaw dropped. "Are you serious? Why not?"

I told her about the situation he had just come out of with the woman who had claimed that he was the father of her baby and his reaction to it.

"He'll think that I'm doing the same thing too," I said.

Linda was quiet for a few seconds. "I can see how you would reach that conclusion but it doesn't matter what he thinks. This is not about you or him. It's about an innocent child who deserves to know who his or her father is."

STEPHEN

I stare at the computer screen trying to make sense of the figures in front of me. It's not rocket science and at a glance, I should be able to tell how each of our franchises is doing in terms of sales and profitability.

But my attention keeps straying. Since the wedding, I've been glancing at my phone every few minutes. Maria has not called and the only times she has texted was to let me know that she's busy. I knew that our affair would come to an end but I never expected it to end this abruptly and without a sign.

We had had so much fun at Paige's wedding and afterwards, she had been looking forward to continuing the evening at my place. What could have gone wrong and made her change so drastically?

I knew that she was physically fine. I'd walked past the bakery in a moment of desperation and seen her behind the counter. She was choosing not to see me and that fucking hurt. I wouldn't have thought that Maria had it in her to be so cold. She reminded me of myself when I made up my mind to end things with a woman.

For the first time, I was on the receiving end of my behavior and it was fucking awful. The smart thing would have been to forget about Maria and move on with my life. The only problem was that I couldn't stop thinking about her.

It felt as if color had been stripped from my world. Not only that, but my world had tilted to one side and nothing made sense anymore. I had to see her one more time. I deserved an explanation on why she had suddenly shut me out.

That decided, I was able to settle back to work, even though I spent more time analyzing her bakery more than the others. It was doing superbly well and sales had soared. Maria's website was up and running and she had told me that they were getting a lot of their custom orders through the website.

That evening, I timed myself to get to the bakery after closing hours. I had my driver drop me off and then dismissed him for the rest of the evening. The front door was shut as I had expected and I walked around to the service door at the back.

It was slightly ajar and I pushed it the rest of the way and entered. The scent of baked goods wafted up my nostrils and I sniffed at it appreciatively. Maria was not in the kitchen but seconds later, the door that led to the front of the bakery opened and she entered.

She grinded to a halt when she saw me. "You startled me."

I had missed that voice. "I'm sorry." I was so happy to see her that for a second, I could only stare at her. My heart felt as if it had been ripped open, bared for the world to see. "You haven't been responding to my messages."

She stared at me and didn't say a word. What the hell was going on with her?

I tried to approach it from another angle. "How have you been?"

She blinked rapidly before answering. "I've been just fine." She looked tired, as if she hadn't been sleeping well.

My heart squeezed painfully with the need to take away her pain or whatever else that was bothering her.

"Sit down. I'll make you some tea," I said expecting her to refuse. To my surprise, she nodded and went and sat down.

All our kitchens were laid out the same, irrespective of the side and I easily found my way around to cook the tea. I could feel Maria's stare following me around the kitchen until it was ready and I set the mug on the table.

"Thank you," she said and wrapped her hands around the mug as if needing its warmth.

I'd made myself a mug of coffee as well and for a few minutes, we sipped our drinks without speaking.

"Something is wrong, right?" I asked her.

She nodded, a vulnerable look coming over her features. Every instinct in me urged me to go to her and hold her. But I needed to know what was going on with her. If that chance passed, I had a feeling that she would close up and the opportunity would be lost.

"What is it?" I asked her softly.

She swallowed hard and then licked her lips. She exhaled before speaking. "I'm pregnant."

I had known that it would eventually happen but actually hearing that made me feel as if a clock had started ticking. Then another thought hit me. "You had said that nothing would change between us. Have you changed your mind?"

None of it made any sense. Why did she look so downcast that she was pregnant and it's what she had wanted all along?

"I didn't get the procedure done," Maria said.

I didn't understand. For two seconds, then I got it and everything in me went still. If I was correct, Maria was pregnant with my baby. Fuck. I searched her face. She looked absolutely miserable and while I didn't expect her to be excited, it hurt that the thought of being pregnant with my baby made her feel that way.

"We barely know each other," she said. "And we were just having some adult fun together."

Adult fun? I'd have laughed if something had not been squeezing my chest. "We got careless." I can't remember the last time I'd worn a condom when having sex with Maria.

"I've only been with you," she said.

"I know." It hadn't even crossed my mind to question whether the baby was mine.

"I don't want anything from you. I just wanted you to know," she said. "I can raise my baby alone and I can definitely provide for him or her."

I gaped at her. "Are you serious? You just expect me to walk out of here and move on with my life as if I don't have a baby on the way? I'm not a sperm donor Maria. We're in this together and I'm going to be there every inch of the way."

"I don't want you to do it from a sense of duty," she said.

"It is my responsibility," I said. What was the matter with her? If she thought she was going to get rid of me that easily, she had another thing coming.

"How did you find out?" I asked her.

"The clinic called Amber to tell her. That's why she wanted to see me on the evening after the wedding," Maria said. "She wanted me to give the baby to her and Jack when it's born."

My jaw tightened. "No one is taking my baby."

"I know, I told her," Maria said. "She hasn't spoken to me since."

I'd not met Amber but from what I heard about her, I wasn't sure I wanted to meet her. With the baby coming, I'd get to meet Maria's family, because like it or not, we were all bound together by the baby.

"I'm sorry," Maria said. "I know that a baby is not part of your plans."

"Don't be sorry. We were both responsible." I should have been spitting saliva with anger, but what I felt was happiness. I wanted to announce it to the whole world, that I was expecting a baby. But I couldn't show it to Maria knowing how she must have been feeling about being saddled with my baby when she had been ready to be pregnant with her sister's baby.

"I have to go. I'm tired and I want to go up to rest," Maria said and stood up.

"Okay," I said and carried the dirty mugs to the sink. I rinsed them while she finished up, then we left together.

"I'll talk to you soon," I said and waited until she shut the door.

I grinned like a fool and then fished out my phone. I found Jeremy's number and hit dial. "Hey man," I said after we exchanged greetings. "Do you want to go for a quick drink?"

"Sure," he said and we agreed to meet at The Blue bar.

Rather than take a cab, I decided to walk to the bar. It was fifteen minutes away and for once, I was not in a rush. I was going to be a father. In several months, there would be a little human being who would call me dad.

Jeremy was already seated at the bar counter when I got there. I clapped his shoulder and slid onto the bar stool next to him. The bartender came and asked for my order.

"I'll have a cold beer as well," I said.

"A cold beer coming up," the friendly bartender said.

"This is a first," Jeremy said. "You suggesting a drink on a week day."

"It's not just a drink," I said, unable to keep an idiotic grin from my face. "it's a celebration."

"Oh. What are we celebrating?" he said.

The bartender brought my beer and poured some into the large glass. "Enjoy."

"Thanks."

"I'm on tenterhooks here," Jeremy said. "Is it a business deal?"

"Nothing to do with business. It's personal," I said. "I'll start at the beginning. I've been seeing this beautiful, wonderful woman. Her name is Maria and she owns one of our franchises."

"I didn't know you were seeing someone," Jeremy said.

I threaded my fingers through my hair. "That's because we were not exactly seeing each other. It wasn't a relationship."

"Ah I see," Jeremy said. "You were fucking her."

"No," I protested the vulgarity of the word. "Okay yes but it was more than that. We're friends. Adult fun is how she refers to it." I chuckled as the memory of Maria saying that came to me.

"Go on."

"Anyway, here's where it gets complicated. She was about to surrogate for her sister when she found out that she was pregnant with my child," I said.

"You look pleased," Jeremy said. "Unlike the last time a woman told you that she was pregnant with your child."

"That's because I knew that she was lying," I said.

"How can you be sure that Maria is telling the truth?"

I'd been expecting that question from Jeremy. "Because we'd been having sex almost every day and there was no one else for either of us. Trust me on that one. She wasn't planning on telling me either but I sort of cornered her into coming clean."

"I believe you," Jeremy said. "You're the most cynical asshole I know. If you say the baby is yours, then it is."

"I'm excited Jeremy. I never wanted a baby but now that Maria is pregnant, I feel as if it's the one thing I've wanted all my life."

"It's a good feeling to be a dad," Jeremy said. "Makes you look at life differently."

"I'm already thinking differently," I said and laughed.

"Your mom will be happy. Maybe this will get her off your back," Jeremy said.

"The only thing that would get her off my back is marriage," I said. Then an idea came to me. An idea so perfect it would sort out all our problems. "What if I asked Maria to marry me?"

Jeremy stared at me skeptically. "These days, women don't get married simply because they're pregnant. They marry for love."

Maria did not love me and as for me, I liked her a whole lot and I did have feelings for her. "We'd both benefit from getting married. It would get my mother off my back once and for all and for Maria, she and the baby would be secure."

"I don't know. You'd vowed to never get married again after Paige," Jeremy reminded me.

"Yeah, but that was before I became a dad."

MARIA

"**M**y feet are killing me," Beth said as we sat sipping coffee and tea in the waiting area of the bakery.

It was our slowest time of the day and I'd asked Beth to have tea with me. I'd started to really get used to the idea of being a mother and had even made an appointment with an obstetrician for that Monday.

"Mine too," I said.

"You look a little better now," she said. "Must have been fatigue."

"I feel better but it wasn't fatigue," I told. "I'm pregnant."

"Already?" she shrieked. "Girl, you are fertile."

I giggled. "I probably am but it's not what you think." I told her about Stephen being the dad.

"That baby is going to be loaded," Beth said.

"Don't be crass," I snapped. That was the very thing I was worried about. People were going to think that I'd gotten pregnant with Stephen's baby because of his bank account and his family wealth.

I didn't even want to think about what his mother would think and say. I would hate her to think that I'd gotten pregnant deliberately. I could just imagine the disappointment she would feel when she learned that I was pregnant. She had sent Stephen to me to give me pointers on how to make the bakery profitable.

"Sorry," Beth quipped. "Congratulations. You're going to be a mom! You'll love it and you'll be a great mom."

"Thanks," I said, her enthusiasm contagious. "I'm spending some sleepless nights worrying about whether I'll be able to balance my work and the baby."

"You will because you have to. Luke has taught me that I can do a lot more than I think. It will be exhausting but rewarding too," she said. "How did Stephen take it?"

I smiled. "Very well actually. I made sure to make him understand that I was just informing him and he wasn't under any obligation to play an active role in raising the baby."

"And?" Beth prodded.

"He reacted as if I had lost my mind to even suggest such a thing," I said, smiling at the memory. "He wants to be a present dad."

"You have that going for you as well," Beth said. "Everything will be just fine."

My spirits fell as I remembered the one person who was terribly unhappy about the whole business. Amber. "My sister will never speak to me again."

"She'll get over it," Beth said. "You were willing to do it which is more than Linda was. Besides, sometimes things work out for the best. You probably weren't ready to act as a surrogate. Most women who do already have their own families."

"Yeah, you're right," I said.

Getting Beth's perspective helped me with mine and put to rest the things that were worrying me. There was nothing I could do about letting Amber down. What happened had happened. We all just had to deal with it.

Later in the evening, as I was preparing a chicken salad dinner in my apartment, the buzzer rang and my heart skipped a beat. I hurried to the front door and pressed the speaker.

"Hi Maria, it's me. Stephen."

My legs turned to jelly. I'd missed him so much in the last two days. I pressed the button to open the downstairs door. "Come on up." I opened the front door as heavy footsteps sounded on the stairs.

"Hi," I said when he appeared on the landing.

"Hi," Stephen said. "Can I come in?"

"Yes, of course." I held the door and as he went by, his masculine cologne permeating the space, reminding me of happier, simpler days.

He crossed the living room in two long strides and sat down. "Can I get you anything?"

"No, I'm fine, thanks. I was hoping we could talk a bit more," he said a look of uncertainty crossing his features.

We were being so formal and it was killing me inside. I missed the carefree Stephen I knew. The one I had fun with. My unexpected pregnancy had caused this barrier between us.

"Sure," I said and sat down facing him.

"This is something that I've given a lot of thought to and I hope you will too before giving me an answer," he said, looking solemn.

"Okay." I drummed my fingers on my thighs. Whatever it was he wanted to say did not sound good.

"I want us to get married."

My jaw dropped. I had expected anything else but that. He might as well have told me that he wanted us to go to space. My heart pounded rapidly as my brain tried to work out why he would think of marriage.

"I want my baby to have a secure future," Stephen continued. "I want him or her to grow up in a family with parents who are married to each other."

It started as a little seed of pain, and it expanded with every passing second. What of love or even affection? I'd always believed that when I did get married, it would be to a man I was insanely in love with and who felt the same about me.

What Stephen was suggesting was a business arrangement. I agreed that it would be good for our baby but I wanted my dream. There was also the issue of our families. My family already knew that Stephen and I were not serious about each other. What would they think if they heard that we now wanted to get married?

And Mrs. Cohen. Blood drained from my face when I thought about the woman who had given me a chance in business. "What will your mom say?"

Stephen stared at me. "My mother? What does she have to do with this? We're adults Maria and we can make our own decisions."

"Even so, I'd hate it if she thought it was a deliberate move on my part," I said weakly.

A hard look came over his features. "What matters is what I think and that thought has never crossed my mind."

It didn't make me feel any better.

"If you like, we can tell her together. I'm going over there for dinner tomorrow. Come with me. She's always asking about you."

Everything was moving so fast. Marriage? "Maybe we can tell her about the baby but not the other part," I said. "I'm not sure I want to get married for the reasons you cited."

"I understand. Just think about it, okay?" he said. "It would mean a lot to me to know that you and the baby are taken care of should anything ever happen to me."

To my embarrassment, I burst into tears. Noisy, ugly crying. A strong arm went around my waist, lifting me up from my chair. The next thing I knew, I was on Stephen's lap with my hands thrown around his neck.

"It's okay," he said. "Everything will be fine. I promise. I'm right here and I'm not going anywhere."

His words made me cry harder. "I miss you," I said, when I was able to speak.

"I missed you too so much," he said, holding me tighter.

He held me until the tears subsided and then he gently wiped the tears on my cheeks with the back of his hand. He cupped my face and hit me with a kiss that set fire to my heart.

God. I had missed his kisses. I raked my fingers through his hair and moaned into his mouth. I dropped my hands to his shoulders and back. I wanted to touch him everywhere.

"I want to kiss you everywhere," he said and stood up taking me with him.

I wrapped my legs around his waist and as we moved to my bedroom, I sucked his tongue and grinded against his erection. In the bedroom, he gently lowered me to the floor and in the frenzy of activity that followed, clothes flew everywhere as we stripped off each other's clothes.

"Your breasts are bigger and softer," Stephen said, holding them in his large hands as if to weigh them. "I've dreamed of making love to you when you're carrying my child every night and woken up with a painful erection every morning."

I laughed. "I can't believe you're here. I thought we were done."

"I'm glad I'm here," he said and lowered his head to suck a nipple.

I groaned deeply as he sucked it and twirled his tongue around it, teasing it mercilessly.

"You're nipples have become bigger too," he growled. "I love them like this."

"Oh God," I said. "They're a hundred times more sensitive now. I could come just from what you're doing."

"Fuck Maria. I want to come from your words…and your body. I've missed this."

He moved from one nipple to another, pleasuring me and soon I needed to lie down as my legs were growing weak with arousal. I tugged at him and he stood up and gathered me into his arms, holding me close and crushing my breasts against his chest.

His steel hard cock pressed against my belly, jerking back and forth. His hands cupped my ass and then stroked me everywhere he could reach.

"Bed," I said and moved to the bed. I lay flat on my back and Stephen followed me and lifted my legs to his shoulders. I trembled from anticipation and when his mouth found my clit, I screamed. Every part of me had become ultra-sensitive, the pleasure alternating between unbearable to not nearly enough.

"Oh Steven." The emotions of the last couple of weeks came to the surface at the same time as my body exploded with an orgasm and I sobbed noisily as I came.

"These are tears of joy," I said to a startled Stephen. "I want you," I said in between my sobs.

"Okay," he said. "This is weird but hot. You sure it's okay to do this when you're pregnant?"

"Double sure," I said.

He gently lowered my legs and then bent his head to kiss my belly. That got me crying again.

"I'm a mess," I said.

"My mess," Stephen said as he guided his cock to my entrance.

It felt like the first time when his cock prodded the slick folds of my pussy and then pressed in. His cock felt thicker than usual and I felt as if it was going to tear me apart, but in a delicious way.

"Are you okay?" he asked when he was halfway in.

"Is it possible to die from pleasure?" I said.

He chuckled. "You'll be the first and I'll be a close second."

He plunged into me the rest of the way and I was sure I'd died and gone to heaven. I wrapped my legs around his waist, drawing him deeper.

"You're so fucking beautiful and sweet," Stephen said, his voice rugged and sweat dripping down the sides of his face.

"Fuck me, Stephen. I've missed this so much," I said unashamedly.

He pulled his cock out slowly and then buried it back in. Tears escaped from the corners of my eyes. We moved together in a perfect rhythm, with me raising my hips to meet every thrust.

His gaze moved from my face to my bouncing breasts. I loved the passionate, hungry look in his eyes as he stared at me. It made me feel sexy and wanted. He supported himself with one hand and used the other to tug on my nipples. That was the last straw for me.

The orgasm ripped through me like bolts of electricity. My legs turned to water as I squeezed Stephen harder.

"Oh yes babe, come for me," he said, using an endearment for the first time. "You look so hot, so wild when you're coming."

I squeezed my inner muscles together and Stephen growled. I did it again and he grunted and called out my name. He drove into me harder as he spilled his seed into me and his cock throbbed deep inside.

We panted for a few seconds and then our breathing slowly returned to normal. Stephen withdrew and came to lie beside me. I lay my head on his chest and listened to the sound of his heart, feeling at peace.

The future didn't seem so frightening when I lay in his arms like that. We would face it together.

MARIA

It was my turn to shut down the bakery and when I did, I hurried upstairs to get ready for dinner at Mrs. Cohen's. Stephen's scent still lingered in the bathroom and as I showered memories of the morning came to me, putting a smile on my face.

Stephen had spent the night and, in the morning, I'd woken up slowly so as not to wake him up and then padded into the shower. A minute later, he had followed me in and insisted on washing me. After the shower, he had coaxed me back to bed, insisting that he needed to check whether he had done a good job cleaning me.

We had spent the morning in bed and had only gotten up when my time to go to work got closer and my stomach growled with hunger. My body remembered the morning and my nipples became hard bullets on my chest. I played with them, imagining that my fingers were Stephen's.

I snaked a hand between my legs and rubbed a finger up and down my clit. I moaned softly and increased the speed and pressure. Needing more, I inserted a finger into my pussy, and pumped in and out, all the while rubbing circles on my clit with my thumb.

I whimpered as the coil of delicious tension shot from my pussy to the rest of my body. My toes curled in pleasure as the orgasm edged near and I moved my finger faster and rubbed my clit harder.

My pussy clenched around my finger as I came and I let out a series of whimpers. As the wave webbed away, I leaned heavily on the bathroom wall. Reality hit me hard. We were going to tell Mrs. Cohen that I was pregnant with her grand-child when she hadn't even known that there was something going on between Stephen and me.

I felt like hiding myself in my bathroom and never leaving.

I scrubbed myself down, washing away the residues of my arousal and then rinsed myself off. I got out of the shower, dried myself and padded naked to the bedroom.

I'd chosen black pants and a cream blouse for the evening. I didn't want to tempt Stephen in any way, knowing that all he had to do was to touch me and the next minute I'd be begging him to fuck me.

I finished getting ready and sat in the living room twirling my fingers as I waited for Stephen to come. He rung the buzzer at six and I grabbed my light jacket and purse and left.

"I'm still not sure that this is a good idea," I told Stephen as I got into his car.

He banged the door shut and went around to the driver's side. "How did I know you were going to say that?" he said. "Relax, you'll be okay and so will my mother. Don't forget what I told you. We're adults and we make our own decisions."

"I know I know," I said.

"Tell me something interesting that happened to you today," Stephen said as he drove.

"Mmmmm, let me see." Nothing came to mind from my work day so I settled for the last half hour. "I touched myself in the bathroom just now and fantasized that it was you doing it."

Stephen choked on his saliva. "I definitely never expected that. How wet were you?"

"Extremely wet," I said, enjoying the game. "Arousal juices were dripping down my thighs."

"Fuck," Stephen said in an affected voice. "I'm so hard right now, I'm tempted to pull over to the side of the road and fuck you in the car."

Heat flooded my body at the vision his words created. "We'll put that down on our bucket list."

He chuckled. "I like having a sexual bucket list."

We flirted all the way to his mother's house. She lived in an obviously wealthy gated neighborhood, with houses set so far from the road that you couldn't see them.

Butterflies fluttered in my belly. "I'm scared."

Stephen took my hand. "Don't be. I'm right here. We've done nothing wrong. We're just two people who happen to have insane chemistry which has resulted in conception. Besides, she's always asking for grandchildren."

I'd heard that wealthy people liked to marry from their own circles. What if Mrs. Cohen was like that? What sort of relationship would we have if she was disappointed that Stephen and I were having a baby together?

The car came to a stop in front of a massive house with gorgeous pillars at the front. For a few seconds, my nervousness dissipated as I admired the house. "Did you grow up here?"

"Yes," Stephen said. "I only realized how big it was after I'd moved out.

"Was it lonely?" I couldn't imagine living in such a place as a kid. In comparison, my childhood home resembled a bathroom.

"No, you'll see what you I mean when we go in," Stephen said. "There are more workers than furniture in my mother's house. It's always been."

We got out and he took my hand as we walked up to the front door. He rang the bell which resembled a church bell. A minute or so passed by before the door swung open and a uniformed maid stood there.

"Mr. Stephen," she said and stood to the side to let us in.

I followed Stephen into the house and found myself in a huge foyer that was as big as my living room.

"Your mother is in the drawing room," the maid said.

We walked down a hallway and passed another uniformed maid who nodded at us. I understood what Stephen had said about his mother's home having a lot of workers.

Mrs. Cohen stood up when she saw me and a genuine smile of delight came over her features when she saw me. My chest tightened with guilt. She had helped me start my bakery and how did I repay her? By sleeping with her son and then getting pregnant.

"Maria? What a pleasant surprise," Mrs. Cohen said pulling me into a warm hug. "Stephen, you should have told me that Maria was coming?"

"I wanted it to be a surprise," Stephen said, kissing his mother's cheek.

"It's a wonderful surprise," she said. "Sit, let's talk a while before we go for dinner." She took my hand and pulled me down to sit next to her. "I've invited you for dinner a few times and each time you said no. So now, Stephen will be my secret weapon when I want you to come."

I laughed. "I should have come." It was true that she had invited me several times to her place for lunch or dinner. I remember thinking at the time that I didn't want to become too close with her as she was sort of my boss.

Now, I was not only close to her, I was carrying her grandchild.

Another uniformed maid came and offered us drinks. I stuck to water as did Stephen. Mrs. Cohen was nursing a glass of sherry.

She asked me about work though I could tell that Stephen had kept her up to date on the goings on at the bakery. We chatted for fifteen minutes or so and then it was time for dinner.

We walked into an adjoining formal dining room with a table that could easily sit twenty people. It had been set on one end, Stephen and I sat on either side and Mrs. Cohen sat at the head.

Nausea swirled in my belly. I wasn't sure how I was going to keep anything down. Stephen had said that we would tell her after dinner. I managed to look as if I was eating by forking tiny pieces of food.

"Did you enjoy the food Maria?" Mrs. Cohen said when we finished dessert.

"It was very tasty and filling, thank you," I said.

We moved to the drawing room and again I refused the offer of wine or coffee and instead asked for water. My heart pounded hard in my chest, knowing that the moment was minutes away. I admired Stephen for how calm he was considering the bomb he was about to drop.

He waited until we were alone again. "Mother, there's a reason why I invited Maria for dinner."

"There need not be a reason for inviting Maria. You know you're welcome here anytime, my dear."

I forced a smile. "Thank you." My voice was trembling.

"Maria is pregnant with my child," Stephen said bluntly.

Mrs. Cohen gasped. "Stephen! What did you do?"

The question would have been funny had the situation not been so dire.

"I trusted you with Maria," Mrs. Cohen continued.

"Mother—" Stephen started to say.

"Mrs. Cohen, we were both responsible," I said. "Stephen didn't force me into anything. I knew what I was doing and I admit that there was some carelessness involved."

She shook her head. "I blame you Stephen. You're a worldly man and you should know better than that. But what is done is done. What do you plan to do about it?"

"I'll take care of Maria and the baby," Stephen said unperturbed by his mother's disappointment and blame.

She squared her shoulders. "You'll do more than that. You'll do right by Maria. She will not have a child out of wedlock."

"Mrs. Cohen, that won't be necessary," I protested.

She continued as if I hadn't spoken. "It'll be a small ceremony with only close family and friends before the baby starts showing. We won't taint Maria's reputation."

"Mother," Stephen said. "We're not in the dark ages. No one's reputation gets tainted because of having a child out of marriage."

"In my circle, they do," Mrs. Cohen said. She turned to me and smiled. "Everything's going to be okay my dear, you're not to worry about a thing. We'll take care of you."

I was at a loss for words. Mrs. Cohen had cast me as the innocent party and Stephen as the villain. We left soon after, amid promises to invite my family for dinner so that everyone would get to know each other before the wedding.

The reality of the situation hit me as we were driving home. "Getting married is crazy Stephen."

"Why? It sounds perfect for me. In addition to giving you security, it will get my mother off my back. I've never told you this, but she arranges for me to date her friends' daughters almost every other week."

I laughed. "Have you really gone on arranged dates?"

Stephen nodded. "More times than I can count. You'll be doing me a favor too if you agree to marry me. Look, I know I'm not who you had in mind for a future partner, but we can make it work."

I liked his honesty and the way he said it made me think that maybe we could make it work and maybe with time, we could grow to love each other.

For me, the foundation was already there. I'd never met a man who affected me as strongly as Stephen did.

I inhaled deeply as the idea of getting married to Stephen took root. It dawned on me that he had not met anyone in my family. If we were going to go ahead with it, then I needed to take Stephen home to meet my family.

STEPHEN

I replaced the formal jacket I'd worn after my shower with a casual one. I studied my reflection. I looked casual smart. I ran a hand through my hair and gave myself one last look over. It wasn't every day that a man was introduced to the family of the woman he was going to marry.

With Paige, it had been different because our families knew each other and had moved in the same circles especially when my father had been alive. There had been no formal meet the family dinner.

I knew no one from Maria's family except in name but they had to be great people seeing the kind of person they had raised. I grabbed my keys and left my apartment. I coasted the SUV onto the road and drove to Maria's apartment.

It was unbelievable that we'd known each other for less than two months and now we were about to tie the knot. On paper it seemed like a careless thing to do but in reality, it made perfect sense. I wanted my child to be secure whether I was there or not and that went for Maria as well.

My mother had unwittingly aided me in my mission when she demanded that I make an honest woman of Maria. Had she not insisted on that, I doubt that Maria would have wanted to marry me. She was a romantic at heart and I suspected she had always hoped for a romantic man for a life partner.

I had no romantic bone in my body but I planned on treating her like a queen every day of our lives and ensuring she never lacked for anything. I had strong feelings for her and the more time we spent together, the more those feelings increased.

As for the baby, I had my moments of insecurity. I'd been raised by an absent dad and I remember longing for him and questioning my mother why he was never home. The answer was always 'work'. I grew up believing that work was more important to my father than I was.

When I became a man though, I understood him better as I was cut from the same cloth. I loved my work. Adrenaline rushed through me when I came across a company with a lot of potential. While other people dreaded Mondays, I loved them and I could happily spend a month at work, stopping only to shower and eat.

Paige had been right at the time that I'd have made a lousy father. Not now though. I didn't want that for my child. I didn't want them to ever think that I loved my work more than I loved them. I vowed to always make time for my family however exhilarating or exciting work was.

Maria allowed me to park in front of her building after work hours since none of her employees were there to see me.

That would end soon. I couldn't wait to introduce Maria as my wife to everyone.

To know that every night, I would go home to her and wouldn't have to sneak out of her apartment in the wee hours of the morning before the bakery opened. It struck me how odd it was that I should be so excited about a marriage of convenience.

I killed the engine and got out of the car. As I strolled up to the apartment building, it struck me that if things went according to plan, Maria would have to give up her apartment and come and live with me. Marriage came with a lot of decisions but we were both reasonable people and I was sure it would be a smooth transition.

I hit the buzzer and Maria's voice came over the speaker.

"I'll be down in a sec honey," she said.

Warmth flooded me at her affectionate tone. "I could be a thug you know."

"But you're not," her laughing voice said.

I waited for another minute before the door swung open and Maria stepped out. She came to me and threw her hands around my neck.

"Hello babe," I said, the endearment falling easily out of my mouth. I kissed her mouth and cheek and trailed more kisses down to her neck.

She laughed as it got ticklish. "You smell so good."

"So do you," I said. "Ready?" I took her hand and led her to the SUV. I opened the passenger door with flourish. "At your service."

She giggled. "Thank you. You make me feel very posh."

"You are posh and beautiful," I said and banged the door shut.

I sprinted around the car and entered the driver's side.

"You're energetic today," Maria said.

"More like nervous energy," I admitted and turned the ignition key. I was both excited and nervous. Maria inputted her parents' address in the car's GPS.

"You shouldn't be. They'll love you," Maria said. "I'm the one who should be nervous. I'd told them about you and said that we're not serious. Now, we're planning to get married. I'll sound insane."

I laughed at the picture of herself she painted, a complete opposite of who she was. "Tell me about them."

"You'll either love Linda or hate her. She speaks her mind, which can be a blessing or a curse. Amber is charming when she wants to be and you'll love her. Forget what I told you about her. Keep an open mind and you'll like her. Jack is just sweet and kind. There's nothing not to like about him."

"What about your parents?"

"They're parents I guess," she said in a bored tone which made me chuckle.

"You're about to become a parent yourself," I reminded her. "Would you like it if your child used that tone to describe you?"

She grinned. "You have a point there. My dad is the quiet type and when he does talk, we all pay attention. My mother is the spokesperson and we don't always see eye to eye."

"She sounds like my mother," I quipped.

Maria laughed. "She's nothing like your mother. Well maybe a little. She likes giving orders too."

We drove to Maria's old home, in a middle-class neighborhood with tree lined streets and well-kept houses with nice sized lawns at the front. We came to a stop at the very end of the street in front of a cream and brown colored house.

"This is home," Maria said. "We moved here when I was thirteen. I loved having friends as neighbors."

"Are you still in touch with them?" I asked her.

"No, we lost touch when people went off to college. My circle has grown smaller as the years go by. My sisters are my best friends and Keziah and Beth at the bakery are close friends too."

"I guess that does happen when people become adults. Jeremy is my lawyer but he's also my best friend. We grew up together," I said.

"I'd like to meet him someday," Maria said.

"You will."

Maria and I got out of the car and walked up to the house and up the steps to the porch. She flashed me a reassuring smile and then rang the bell. She was about to ring it again when the door was answered.

A woman who could only be Maria's sister stood at the door. She looked at me in surprise, a sharp reminder that Maria had decided to do as I had done and not warn her family that she was bringing me along for the family dinner.

"I didn't know we were having a guest for dinner," she said.

"No one does," Maria said. "Stephen, this is my sister Linda."

Linda squealed. "I've heard loads about you," she said turned to me. "He's dishy."

"Stop it," Maria said.

I laughed. "I've heard loads about you too." I shook her hand. "It's a pleasure to meet you."

"Come on in," she said and we followed her.

Everyone was in the living room and when they saw me, they all stood up. Maria performed the introductions and I didn't miss the questioning look her mother gave her when she thought I wasn't looking.

After the initial welcome, her father fell silent and sat observing everything without chipping in.

"This is the first time that Maria has brought a man home," Linda said. "But I guess you're not just any man. You're the father of her baby."

"Yes, and I've been looking forward to meeting all of you," I said smoothly.

"That's actually the reason I brought Stephen over. We have some news we want to share with you," Maria said, surprising me.

I'd expected her to wait until after dinner before diving in. I made a mental note to teach her that strategy for future use. If you had some news that you weren't sure of how it would be received, wait until you were almost leaving. That way, if it went badly, you didn't have to endure an uncomfortable dinner.

Everyone turned to Maria and looked at her expectantly.

"Well," she started and flashed me a smile. "Stephen asked me to marry him and I said yes."

Everyone gasped except for Jack. They all stared at Maria and then me.

"I count myself a very lucky man because she said yes," I said to fill in the heavy silence which had fallen around us.

"You two are practically strangers from what Maria said," Amber said. "Why would you get married?"

"Honey," Jack said in a tone laced with a warning.

"I'm just asking what everyone is thinking," Amber said.

"I think it's a good idea," Maria's mom finally said. "Every child deserves to be born in the warmth of a family. You're doing the right thing Stephen."

"Thank you, Mrs. Swan," I said, relief surging through me. I let out a breath I hadn't known I'd been holding.

Mr. Swan stood up and came to where I was seated. He offered his hand and I jumped to my feet.

"Welcome to the family," he said.

"Thank you."

Jack did the same and the ladies hugged me, albeit a little awkwardly.

"Well," Mrs. Swan said. "This looks like a celebration. Let's go and have dinner. I'm sure we can find a bottle of wine to toast to the engaged couple."

"Do you have a ring yet?" Linda said.

"Not yet," Maria said.

"She'll have it in a couple of days." I'd completely forgotten about the engagement ring.

As everyone got up to go to the dining room, Jack and I lagged behind.

"Congratulations again," he said. "Maria is a great girl and you two will be very happy together."

"Thank you," I said, touched by his words. Maria had been right. Jack was a good man.

"Listen," he continued, throwing a glance at the door through which everyone else had disappeared. He moved closer. "About the surrogacy thing, please know that Amber and I are completely fine with the way things have turned out."

I nodded, not sure how to respond.

"To be honest, I wasn't very comfortable with the idea. I don't understand what the rush is. I keep telling Amber we can wait and save up for IVF. We're still young and there's time to get a baby down the road."

"I'm glad you feel that way," I said, admiring his brutal honesty. "Things have a way of working out for the best. Your family will grow at the right time."

He nodded. "Absolutely." He draped an arm around me and we walked towards the dining room. "So, I hear that you're an investor. Any tips to share with someone who wants to start investing?"

I grinned. I was at home as long as we were talking investments. "Plenty."

MARIA

"You and Jack really hit it off," I said to Stephen as we drove homewards.

"I like him a lot," he said. "I like all of your family actually. Even the frighteningly forthright Linda."

I laughed. "You did well with them." I grew solemn as the seriousness of what we were about to embark on hit me. "I can't believe we're actually going to go ahead with this."

"Everything has just fallen into place. I like that," Stephen said, sounding unperturbed by the whole thing.

It was as if he got married every day. Well, he'd done it once before so it probably wasn't as big a deal to him as it was to me. I liked that my family had reacted fairly well under the circumstances, especially my mom. I'd expected the most resistance from her.

Then there was the lunch that Mrs. Cohen had invited my family to. One little fact they didn't know about Stephen was that he and his mom owned the Creamy Creations brand.

The only person who knew this was Linda and even she had been so engrossed in the topic of investments over dinner that she'd probably forgotten it.

"Jack told me he and Amber were happy for us and that he was pleased with how it's worked out. He wasn't too happy about the idea of surrogacy in the first place."

"Oh," I said, surprised by that. "Amber had implied that Jack was on board with the idea plus he'd been there that first day."

Stephen shrugged. "He loves your sister. Probably went along with it just to make her happy."

"Yeah, and Amber can be pushy," I said.

"Mine or yours?" Stephen said.

I giggled. "Isn't it a little too late to ask that when you're already parking in front of your apartment?"

He laughed softly. I loved Stephen's laugh and I also loved the profile of his face when he was serious. I loved most things about him. And I was having his baby. Warmth and joy came over me. Babies had never been at the top of my list of things to do but how could they have, when I couldn't even find a good relationship?

"Are you okay coming to my place?" he said. "I want to hold you in my arms and fall asleep to the sound of your heartbeat."

Warmth flooded me. "I want that too," I said.

He parked the car and we got out and walked hand in hand to the apartment building door. The night attendant let us in and after exchanging pleasantries with him, we headed to the elevator. I still couldn't get over how fancy his apartment was.

It had its own private elevator and an atmosphere of wealth and serenity.

"You'll be living here soon," Stephen said as we entered his apartment.

I loved the marble floors and the floor to ceilings windows that showed off the stunning view of the city. The meaning of Stephen's words slammed into me and I turned to face him.

"What do you mean, I'll be living here soon," I said.

"We're getting married, remember. Married people live together," he said, his tone tinged with amusement.

It was stupid but I hadn't thought about the practicalities of being married. "I can't live here, what about my work?"

"You can drive to and from work," Stephen said.

I bit my lower lip and frantically thought of an excuse as to why I couldn't drive. There was none. Only the truth would suffice. "I don't drive. I never learned how."

He stepped closer to me and slipped his hands around my waist. "Hey, that's not such a big deal. I can drop you to and from work."

"At three in the morning?" I said.

"I don't care what time it is, I'll do it," Stephen said. "Anything for you."

I inhaled deeply. I'd always had a fear of driving from an accident we'd had when I was younger. My father had been driving and I remember the moment when he lost control of the car, and it had careened off the road at frightening speed.

Since then, I'd had a fear of cars but over the years it had abated, I'd just not gotten around to learning how to drive. "I could learn how to drive," I said tentatively.

"If you like, I can take you out a few times before you get an instructor. A few confidence booster lessons if you like," Stephen said.

"Would you? That would be great," I said.

"There's this open field a few miles from here where my mother used to take me for lessons. It's still there, I'm sure."

We moved to his bedroom as we spoke. "Your mother was the one who taught you how to drive?" I asked him.

"Yes, amongst other things. My father was always too busy with work to find time to teach me stuff." He took off his jacket and slung it on the love seat in the bedroom. "I don't want that kind of life for my son or daughter. I want to do better than my father did."

My heart squeezed as the image of Stephen as a little boy formed in my mind. How lonely it must have been for him, longing for a dad who was there and yet not there. I touched his shoulder. "You'll be an awesome dad."

"Paige was sure I'd make a terrible dad," he said softly.

"That's not what I see," I said. "I see a man who cares greatly for the people he loves and would do anything for them. Your son or daughter will be very lucky to have you as a dad."

A deep noise rose from his throat and he took a step that brought him next to me. "The day you walked into my life was the day my life changed for the better."

I cocked my head to one side. "Technically, you're the one who walked into mine. My office to be specific."

"That is just semantics," he said and lowered his head to kiss me.

I murmured appreciatively at the sensations that flooded me when he captured my lower lip between his teeth and bit on it gently.

"So what do you say about moving in with me?" he said.

I had completely pushed that conversation out of my mind. The thought of moving out of my apartment filled me with fear.

Stephen slid a hand along my jawline. "What are you frightened of? Moving in with me seems to frighten you more than marriage. It should be the other way round."

"Security," I said to him. "My apartment makes me feel secure. It means that I always have a home no matter what else happens in my life."

"That's easy to solve. We'll keep the apartment," Stephen said.

"Is everything easy for you?" I asked him.

"Not everything," he said. "I'm nervous as hell about messing this up. I never thought I'd even consider getting married again, and now I'm about to do it. That scares me."

I met his gaze and saw the fear reflected in his eyes. "We don't have to do it, you know."

"You're not understanding me," Stephen said. "I want to get married to you, more than anything. But I'm worried of hurting you or making a mess of things by not being what you need."

My heart melted. I cupped his face. "You're already everything I need."

He kissed me softly on my lips. The words we were exchanging sounded as if we were a real couple in love about to get married. Anyone listening to us would find it difficult to believe that we were doing it for other reasons besides love.

Stephen brought his hands from my face and undid the buttons of my blouse, all the while keeping his gaze locked on mine. I trembled with anticipation and arousal as his fingers grazed lightly on my skin as he took off the blouse.

I shrugged off my blouse and it dropped to the floor.

"You're so fucking sexy," he murmured as he cupped my breasts over my bra.

My nipples ached for his touch and when he traced them with his thumbs, I let out a gasp.

"They're so sensitive," he murmured as he undid the front clasp of my bra and slipped it off my shoulders.

His gaze hungrily took in my bare breasts before lowering his head to flick my aching nipples with his tongue. Shots of pleasure ran through my body as he licked and sucked each nipple in turn.

"Oh God Stephen," I moaned gripping his head tight. Desperate for him, I pushed his head lower and he went down on his knees and pulled down my skirt.

I stepped out of it and stood with my legs spread apart, my pussy desperately aching for him. He planted kisses along the wide swell of my hips before moving his mouth to my panty clad pussy.

He licked me over the material, the friction of it making me cry out in both ecstasy and need for more.

"You're so wet," he said. "So hot."

Cold air hit the folds of my pussy and I looked down to see that he had pushed my panties to one side and was softly blowing on me. My legs felt as if they couldn't hold me up for another minute.

"Please," I begged, not sure what I was asking for but knowing I need his tongue and fingers to ease the ache deep inside me.

He obliged with his tongue and set off a wild heat in me. I cried out as he lashed out inside me, tantalizing and teasing me.

"Oh God, please," I cried out on repeat mode. My brain was too soaked in pleasure to come up with more words.

Stephen inserted a finger inside me and pumped it in and out just as I had done in the shower when I was masturbating, pretending it was him. Only the real thing felt a million times better.

I panted as he pumped in and out faster and faster and sucked on my clit with his mouth. When the orgasm exploded, I threw my head back and let out a cry that wouldn't have sounded out of place in the woods.

"Oh God," I kept saying, stunned by the strength of the orgasm.

My body trembled even as the orgasm ebbed away. Stephen stood up, took my hand and eased me onto the bed. When I lay flat, he pulled down my panties and tossed them to the floor.

I rotated my hips, enticing him, urging him to take me. A deep growl filled the room then he lined up his cock to my entrance and thrust into me. His cock swelled inside me with every quick, sharp stab. I clung to his shoulders and dug my fingers into his skin.

I whimpered as the pressure inside me slowly grew. I arched my hips and met him thrust for thrust. Stephen pounded me harder and faster, each stroke sending me reeling.

I felt myself start to crumble as the pleasure rippled through me. My eyes rolled back and I gripped him tighter and the most delicious feeling came over me. My muscles tightened, clenching his steel hard cock and Stephen came, shouting my name as he did so.

I writhed in pleasure as he pumped and gushed his release into me. Stephen kissed me as his cock throbbed inside and then grew still.

"You are so fucking amazing," he said, staring down at me.

"You're not so bad yourself," I teased.

"What time does your shift end tomorrow?" I asked her.

"Noon," she said. "I have an early start."

"I have a surprise for you. Pack an overnight bag and no questions asked," he said, putting on a fierce face.

I giggled, excitement building inside me. I was a sucker for surprises. "Now I won't get any sleep trying to figure out where we're going. Give me a clue."

Stephen kissed me again, the scent of his sweat teasing my nostrils like an aphrodisiac.

"No clues."

STEPHEN

I didn't understand myself. I'd made a pact to keep things as they were with Maria. That way, no one would get hurt. Now, I was in my car, being driven to pick her up, take her to the private airstrip to take a private jet to Paris for the weekend. The kind of thing I did when I was dating.

The idea had come to me when we were having sex. An urge to treat her to a fun weekend had taken root in my brain and would not leave. Still, she was going to be the mother of my baby. She deserved to have a good and relaxing weekend.

I'd tried marrying for love and I knew how that went. This time I was being smarter. I was marrying Maria to provide a family environment for my child. Plus, I was not averse to companionship. That was all.

The car pulled up in front of the bakery and I jumped out. A lightness came over my chest as I hit the buzzer. I was really looking forward to the weekend away and most especially of taking Maria to Paris. The passport had been tricky but I'd managed to slip it into our conversation and not give her time to ask questions.

The door buzzed and I pushed it open and entered. I took the stairs two at a time and when I reached the top, her apartment door was already open.

"You really need to tell me where we're going," Maria said, walking into the living room carrying an overnight bag.

She looked so gorgeous in fitted jeans, a sexy cream blouse and a leather jacket slung on her arm. I took the bag and kissed her on the mouth. Her scent surrounded me and her body brushed against mine, making me forget everything except how much I wanted her in my arms.

"You look beautiful," I said. "And my lips are sealed. You'll find out when we get there." She complained but I could see that she was enjoying the mystery.

Paige had hated surprises and wanted to know every detail of the day or evening. It was fun being with someone who loved being surprised. I carried her bag downstairs to the trunk of the car and followed her into the back seat.

"I've never done this," she said, her eyes gleaming.

I took her hand and sandwiched it in mine. "Done what?"

"Took off for a weekend without knowing where I was going. It's fun and crazy," she said and peered out the window.

I laughed. "It's too early to search for clues. We've just left the bakery."

"I know," she said and sat back, getting more comfortable in her seat. "Your mother came by today and now all my employees know that we're getting married. They want to bake us a massive cake."

"I second that," I said.

"Anyway, your mom wanted to talk about the wedding. I tried telling her that we haven't decided on the date but she wouldn't hear of it. She said that between the two of us, we could come up with a suitable date and then she could get the ball rolling."

Maria sounded horrified. I laughed at her expression. "She felt cheated the last time since Paige and I went to Vegas."

"We had decided on a small wedding but from what she was saying, it sounded big. And you'll not believe this but she has several venues lined up for me and you to see."

"My mother is a bulldozer, Maria. It's just that you're only getting to see that side of her now. How do you think she managed to run the company singlehandedly when my father passed away?"

Maria stared at me wide eyed.

"You deserve a nice wedding. Hopefully it'll be your first and last," I said and pinched the bridge of her nose lightly.

"But a big wedding takes time to plan," she protested.

"Not if my mother has a hand in planning it," I said. "She knows all the wedding planners in this town as well as the next. Don't be surprised to get a call from a planner soon."

"It all sounds overwhelming," she said.

"If it gets too much, tell me. I'll get her to back off, okay?"

She nodded. "Okay." Glancing out the window, she noticed

that we had come to a stop and we were in an airfield. She swung her gaze back to me. "We're flying? Of course we are, you told me to carry my passport. Where are we?"

"A private airport and yes we're taking a private jet to a city that you'll fall in love with," I said.

She looked out again.

"Ready?" I said, not sure if she was pleased or overwhelmed or what. Sometimes, Maria was very hard to read. I fervently hoped that she was going to enjoy the trip.

"Okay," she said in a soft voice and opened the door.

I followed her out and took her hand when she paused to stare at the jet right next to us.

"Welcome," Jenna, the steward said.

"After you," I said to Maria.

She hadn't said a word so far and I was getting worried. Had I made a mistake in assuming that she would enjoy being whisked off to Europe for a weekend in Paris?

We entered and settled down on the comfortable cream leather chairs that had been one of the selling points for the jet. The pilot came over and I introduced him to Maria as my fiancée. It felt good to say that. I'd been single for so long that I'd forgotten the warm feeling that came from being one half of a couple.

"Paris is beautiful at this time of year," he said.

Maria's eyes widened. She stared at me questioningly and I laughed, enjoying the look of total shock and delight on her face. The pilot wished us a good flight and disappeared into the cock pit.

"Stephen, we're going to Paris in a private jet?" Maria asked.

"Correct," I said.

"Isn't it terribly expensive? Honestly, lunch in a nice restaurant would have been enough for me."

I'd never had a woman worry about my wallet when I took her on an expensive outing. All they cared about was how much fun they were going to have. The part of my heart that she had already stolen increased.

"Don't worry about that. I can easily afford it and it won't dent my bottom line. I promise."

She studied me skeptically. "If you're sure. We have a baby on the way you know."

I nodded solemnly. "I know. I wanted to treat you to something special. Take you somewhere I was sure you had never gone. You deserve it."

Her eyes welled up with tears. "I've never done anything like this for sure. Thank you."

I reached out and brushed off a tear from the corner of her eye before it fell. "Let's make this a trip to remember, okay?"

She beamed. "Yes! Tell me everything. Where are we staying, what are we going to do tomorrow?"

I laughed. Her excitement was contagious. I told her about the plans I'd made for the following day. The only time she frowned was when I told her about the shopping expedition for designer clothes. In the past, my problem had been women who were only too eager to spend my money.

I had a new problem now. A problem I'd never had. Getting Maria to spend my money.

When the airplane reached cruising speed, we unbuckled our seatbelts and Jenna came by to offer us drinks. Keeping Maria's pregnancy in mind, we both settled for bottles of chilled water.

We chatted easily as we sipped on our drinks. Two hours later, Jenna returned to tell us that dinner was about to be served. It was a four-course meal that had Maria groaning with being too full when we were done.

The flight to Paris took eight hours and halfway through it, Maria fell asleep. I was tempted to wake her up to move to the comfortable bedroom at the back of the plane but I was loath to wake her up in case she was unable to fall asleep again.

I dozed off too and the next time I woke up, it was to someone gently shaking my shoulder.

"We've almost reached out destination," Jenna said to me softly.

"Thank you," I murmured.

I got up and went to the bathroom to freshen up before returning to wake Maria up. She looked so peaceful and so beautiful when she was asleep that I took a minute to just stare at her.

She had become important to me in such a short time and now we were going to get married and be parents together. I made a silent vow to do my damnedest to make her happy. There was no reason not to. Maria was easy to get along with.

If I hadn't closed off that part of my heart that fell in love, I'd say she would be an easy woman to love. I leaned down to her and kissed her warm cheek. She stirred. I kissed the corner of her mouth and this time, her eyes shot open.

"Good evening," I said to her.

She stared at me before recognition dawned and she gave me a smile that made my heart sing.

"Are we there yet?" Maria said, glancing out the window at the dark skies. "And what time is it?"

I checked my watch, Paris time. "Almost three am."

She stretched and excused herself to go to the bathroom. When she returned, Jenna brought us a light breakfast and Maria ate hers with super speed. She stared at me apologetically when she was dabbing at the sides of her mouth with her napkin.

"Sorry. I was starving. I don't know what happened to all that food I ate for dinner," she said with a wry smile.

"The baby needs it to grow," I said and patted her flat stomach. I couldn't wait to touch it when it was nicely rounded.

"Thanks for making me feel better about my greediness," Maria said with a grin.

"It's the truth," I said.

Her features turned serious. "Have you ever done this before? Taken a woman to Paris for a weekend?"

I nodded. "I've taken Paige."

She had hated it and had been stone faced the whole time. That was the last time I surprised her with anything. I didn't want to think about Paige or any other woman. It felt like the first time for me since the romantic, fun weekend I had envisaged that time had not happened.

Jenna came and cleared away the dishes, after which the pilot's voice came over the plane's intercom informing us that we would be landing in the next half hour.

"We're landing in a private jet airport that is close to the city," I said to Maria.

"Thank you for bringing me to Paris," she said.

"You're welcome." I couldn't think of anyone else I'd rather have been with at that moment other than Maria.

The plane landed smoothly and minutes later, it came to a stop. We unbuckled our seatbelts and stood up just as the pilot appeared.

"There's a car waiting to take you to your hotel. Have a good weekend and we'll see you on Sunday," he said and Jenna echoed the same sentiments.

The limo was waiting three steps from the plane. The uniform clad driver opened the door for us and we entered.

"I could get used to this," Maria said with a giggle.

I smiled. "I'm glad you're enjoying it."

MARIA

I understood then why Paris was known as the city of lights. I pressed my nose to the window of the limo as we drove from the airport to our hotel. All the buildings were illuminated, the way a Christmas tree was decorated with sparkling lights.

I felt like a kid again as I looked out at the passing sights. The trees were decorated with lights too. I was glad we had arrived at night so that I would always remember my first view of Paris.

There was guilt in my excitement too. I didn't want to think about how much money Stephen had spent to get us to Paris. I knew that he was a very successful business man but still, I wasn't a woman he was in love with. I was just someone carrying his baby.

I quelled those thoughts and made myself remember that I'd promised myself that I would have as much fun as I could. When was the next time I'd get a chance to travel to Europe in a private jet no less.

We were staying at the Ritz hotel and from the moment we arrived to being escorted to our suite, I felt like a princess. I tried to act sophisticated and not gape at the luxury that surrounded us.

"What do you think?" Stephen said coming to stand behind me. He slipped his hands around my waist.

"It's perfect. Look at that view. It's like daylight." We were standing by the window looking down at the city. "I want to pinch myself to be sure that I'm not dreaming."

"I have a better idea to prove to you that you're not dreaming," Stephen whispered and nuzzled my neck.

A soft moan escaped my mouth when he trailed kisses along my neck. He ran his fingers over my hips, his erection pressing against my ass. Anticipation screamed through me. I felt as if I'd stolen someone else's life.

"You smell like vanilla and chocolate and flowers," Stephen whispered.

I laughed softly. "Probably from the bakery."

"No. It's all you," Stephen said.

His hands rose to cup my breasts, stroking them over my blouse. I moaned and went limp against him as wild sensations shot through me. He rubbed his thumbs over each nipple while stroking the sides of my breasts with his hand.

Needing to touch him, I turned around and looped my hands around his neck. I raised my head and he brought his head down to kiss me.

"How do you feel about making love in Paris?" Stephen said when we stopped for air.

"I've thought of nothing else since we got on the plane," I responded.

He slipped his hands under my hips and carried me to the bed. He undressed me as if I was fragile and when we were both naked, he spent the next hour pleasuring me until I broke my record of coming twice in the space of an hour.

~

"Rise and shine," a familiar voice said, and I cracked open one eye and blinked against the sudden light.

"What time is it?" I said gazing at Stephen. He looked as if he was already dressed for the day.

"Dawn," he said and drew the curtains open. He came to the bed and leaned to kiss my forehead.

"You smell so fresh," I said, burrowing deeper into the luxurious silk bedsheets.

"I've already showered," he said. "We have an early start. I want you to see the Eiffel tower before the crowds gather. I've already drawn a bath for you."

"Thank you." I threw the beddings away and got off the bed, pausing to kiss Stephen's neck. I padded unconsciously towards the bathroom, pulled by the promise of sinking into a bathtub.

I dipped a finger in the three-quarter full bathtub. "Perfect," I murmured just as Stephen strolled into the bathroom.

He stood by the wall and watched me, his gaze hungry and roving over my body. I hoped he would still stare at me the same way when my pregnancy started showing. I sunk into the bubble filled tub and let out a sigh as warmth enveloped me.

"It's so tempting to come in and join you," Stephen said.

I grabbed an armful of foam and made as though to blow it to him. "Life is short. Hop in."

He stared at me for a few seconds, grinned in that sexy way that I loved so much and carefully undressed, folding each item as it came off. My eyes widened at the erection he was already sporting.

I slid forward and he got in behind me. I inched back, his cock pressing against my back. Stephen trailed his fingers up and down my arms raising goose bumps across my skin.

"You're a bad influence," he said, his breath trickling my ear.

"I like being a bad influence where you're concerned," I said, feeling carefree and more relaxed than I had ever been.

He circled his hands to cup my belly. "It's unbelievable that we have a little one growing here."

I covered his hands with mine. "I know. I still don't believe it to be honest but when my belly starts growing, then I will."

"You'll go down in history as the sexiest pregnant woman who ever lived."

I laughed. "I'm all right with not making history."

He rubbed circles across my belly and then his hands rose to my breasts. Cupping them from my ribcage, he slid his fingers in the valley between my breasts and squeezed gently.

I let out a luxurious moan. "Do we really need to see the Eiffel tower at this hour?"

"Yes, we do," Stephen said, his voice husky. "You'll thank me later."

He grabbed the hotel soap and lathered me in all the areas he could reach from behind me, which were considerable. When he was done, he rinsed me off and helped me out of the tub.

"Not fair," I complained as he dried me.

His hands on me had left me with a fire in my pussy and heat in my belly. "I want you."

"You'll have me when we return to the hotel," he said, peppering my shoulder with kisses.

"If you promise," I said and raised my hands in the air for him to wrap the oversize towel around me.

We got dressed and agreed to skip breakfast. Since falling pregnant, I'd started eating breakfast mid-morning, after I'd thrown up a couple of times. Stephen had arranged for a car to drive us to the Eiffel tower and we found the driver waiting at the entrance.

It was the perfect weather for a touristy day, warm but not so hot that it was uncomfortable to walk around. The tower was everything I had read about and more. Indescribable joy came over me as I stood in front of it staring at the tall, beautiful building.

After the Eiffel tower, we had brunch in a street café and had second cups of coffee unhurriedly.

"I haven't had time off like this," Stephen said.

"Me too," I said. "If my sisters could see me now, they would be so jealous."

"How are things with Amber?" Stephen asked.

Sadness came over me. Despite the talk that Stephen had had with Jack, Amber was still freezing me out. I'd texted her a couple of times but each time, she has texted me back with one-word answers.

Only Linda was excited by the new turn of events. Sometimes, I suspected she was even more excited than I was for me. I oscillated between being terrified and happy.

"She's still cold," I said. "How can she be angry with me for being pregnant?"

"She's not angry at you for being pregnant. She's upset because you've killed her dream of a baby," Stephen said.

"I know," I said.

"Give her time," he said. "It usually works for a lot of people. Time softens anger."

"I hope so. I miss her." Despite Amber's weaknesses and we all had them, I missed her. She was funny and she and Linda were my best friends.

We spent the afternoon visiting all the famous touristy spots and returned to the hotel in time for four o'clock tea. Tired from all the activities of the day, Stephen and I went up to our suite after tea. We took a shower together and then slipped into bed to relax before dinner.

I caressed the day-old stubble on his chin. "I had a magical day. Thank you."

"You're welcome," he said, his dark gray eyes on me. "I've never had such a good time either. You're great company."

A pang of longing came over me and I wished that Stephen and I were something more than two people who found each other insanely attractive. I wished he'd look at me the way a man who loved a woman looked at her.

I should have been glad that he was willing to be a present dad to our baby but being with him in Paris had opened me to another side of Stephen. A soft, fun side. An adventurous side. A side of him that was rarely seen back home when he was busy with his work.

As he had said, work means a lot to him. I understood that as I was the same way. Unlike Stephen though, I had space in my life for love.

"You seem so deep in thought," he said, drawing me back to the present. "What were you thinking about?"

"I was thinking how much I'm dreading going home tomorrow," I said, feeling guilty at the small lie. There was no way I was going to expose my weakness to him. I wasn't going to tell him that I wished he loved me.

Stephen would probably laugh in my face.

"Tomorrow is not here yet," he said. "No point thinking about it." He gently tugged the beddings from under my arm and pulled them down exposing my naked body.

I caught my breath at his heated gaze on me.

"I love your body," Stephen said and slid further down so that his face was directly in front of my breasts.

He took a nipple into his mouth and I gasped. My nipples were taut and big and it felt so good to have him shower his attention on them. Stephen's movements were unhurried as he moved from one nipple to another.

A burning desire radiated from my chest to my pussy and soon I was squirming, desperate to feel him inside me.

"So impatient," Stephen murmured when I begged me to fill me up with his cock. "Turn around," he said and I did as he asked, turning to face the wall.

He slipped his hand between my thighs and stroked my pussy. I moaned deeply and squeezed my thighs together, trying to draw the orgasm out. He withdrew his hand and replaced it with his dick.

Stephen pressed the tip of his cock on my slick entrance but instead of pushing it in, he rubbed it up and down, inflaming me further.

"That feels so good," I said, thrusting my ass out, greedy for more friction. "God, I love your cock. So big…"

"And your pussy is made for it. Fits perfectly," Stephen said.

The ache in my pussy grew more and more insistent as he kept teasing me with his cock, flicking my clit with it and pushing it in for an inch and then drawing it out.

"I'm so hard for you babe," Stephen said.

"Do it!" I said. "Fuck me."

He thrust into me hard, without warning and I let out a sharp cry followed by a series of whimpers.

"You're so fucking tight," Stephen said before pulling out again and thrusting into me hard.

He raised my leg in the air and drove his cock into me in a hard, punishing rhythm. My juices made slurping noises each time he hit my core. Need wound itself tightly in my belly and I arched my ass to get his cock deeper.

Then I toppled over the edge and my body jerked and clenched, waves of pleasure washing over me. It was a long, drawn-out orgasm and when it was over, it left me shattered on the bedsheets.

Stephen's orgasm was like an explosion in my pussy, with jets of cum gushing into me, heating me up again. When it was over, we lay with Stephen's hand around me, feeling one with each other and words completely unnecessary.

STEPHEN

"I'm nervous," Maria said as we were driven across town to her first appointment with the obstetrician.

She was a lady and had come recommended by Beth at the bakery.

"What are you nervous about?" I said.

"I don't know," Maria said. "Last night, I had a nightmare that they'd done a pregnancy test and found that I wasn't pregnant after all."

I contemplated the scenario and knew that I'd be disappointed as hell if it happened. "Would that be a relief to you, hypothetically speaking?"

"Strangely enough, no. I'd be disappointed. I'm looking forward to being a mom and a new phase in my life."

Pleasure flooded me. "I'm glad."

"I've done countless other tests since that one at the fertility clinic," she said. "So I know that nightmare was stupid. But still. It'll be nice to hear from Dr. White that all is well.

Adam dropped us at the building where Dr. White's offices were located and we hurried out. I took Maria's hand and we walked into the building. We found her offices easily enough on the first floor.

"Good morning," I said to the woman receptionist. "My fiancée and I have an appointment with Dr. White."

She smiled. "Your names please?"

Maria gave her name and she asked her to have a seat for a few minutes. Maria's hand had become clammy and when we sat down, I squeezed it.

"Everything will be just fine."

She nodded. "Thanks for coming with me."

"I intend to come for all your appointments, pending a disaster like breaking my legs and even then, I'd probably use a wheelchair and still come."

Maria laughed. "I believe you."

By the time the receptionist brought insurance papers and a medical form for us to fill out, Maria was looking a lot more relaxed. After filling them out, the receptionist invited us to enter the doctor's office.

Dr. White was an older woman with short brown hair and spectacles perched on her nose. She smiled and stood up when we entered and shook our hands.

"I'm Maria Swan and this is my fiancé, Stephen," Maria said.

"It's a pleasure to meet both of you," she said. "Please sit down."

We sat down and she proceeded to ask Maria a few questions about her general health and what made her suspect that she was pregnant. Her eyes widened with surprise when Maria told her about the planned surrogacy.

"Well seeing as you've already done a blood test, we'll go straight to the examination room and also do a scan as well," Dr. White said in reassuring tones.

She took us next door where the examination room was and left us so that Maria could change into the paper gown on the bed. I helped Maria out of her clothes and to my shame, my cock stirred when she was down to her bra and panties.

"I'm hard," I whispered to her a she pulled down the gown over her thighs.

Maria laughed. "I'm flattered that you think I'm sexy in a paper gown."

"You would look sexy in anything," I said. I held her hand as she stepped up onto the platform and lay down on the examination bed.

A knock came on the door and a second later, Dr. White walked in.

"Ready?" she said moving to the sink to wash her hands.

"I'm ready," Maria said, her voice a little shaky.

"Good. And don't be nervous, there's absolutely nothing to worry about." She went to stand on the other side of Maria and proceeded to give her a physical examination.

Afterwards, she poured some jelly on Maria's belly which made her yelp.

"Sorry about that, I should have warned you that the jelly would be cold," she said.

"It's okay." Maria's gaze was glued to the computer screen that Dr. White had wheeled up.

"The ultrasound will give us a view of the uterus as well as the placenta and we can get a lot of useful information from that," Dr. White said moving the scanner up and down Maria's belly.

The screen showed a dark grey moving image but no matter how closely I looked I couldn't see anything. Maria voiced my thoughts.

"I can't see the baby," she said.

Dr. White chuckled. "No you can't but if you look here—" she pointed to a blob on the screen. "This is your baby. She or he is the size of a grain of rice."

Maria sniffed and when I looked at her face, I saw that she was crying. I'd been touched too, to know that our baby was in there somewhere, growing bigger by the day.

She reached for my hand and squeezed it.

"Everything is looking good," Dr. White said.

Maria and I exchanged a look of relief. We stayed at the doctors for twenty more minutes and then we left after securing an appointment in a month's time. We were going to meet later in the evening at my mother's place for dinner with both families but when I took her back to the bakery, I held her a little longer than I needed to.

I returned to the dining room where my mother was putting last minute touches to the dining room.

"How are things in the kitchen," she said, looking at me with a smile.

"You know Greg," I said, referring to my mother's chef who had been with the family for decades. "He's a real pro."

My mother stopped what she was doing and contemplated me. "You're uncharacteristically nervous. This is the first time I've seen you come early for dinner to ensure that everything is going smoothly."

"It's an important dinner. These people are going to be family," I said.

She made a non-committal sound. "You love her, don't you?"

I raised my eyebrow in surprise. "Maria? We get along and I want to give my child a home. I was done with love after Paige but I realize that I need to give my child a home."

Even as I said the words, I realized how wrong they sounded. It may have started off like that but after the weekend in Paris with Maria, another chunk of ice in my heart had melted.

I knew that I needed to keep a firmer grip on my feelings. As sweet as Maria was, I couldn't risk going through the kind of pain I'd gone through when Paige and I divorced. The only way to do that was to keep my feelings out of it. See it like the business arrangement it was.

"It saddens me to hear you say that," my mother said. "Your father and I loved each other and because of that, we had a happy marriage. I want that for you too."

"Not everyone can have that," I said. "Besides, father might have been the best husband but he wouldn't have won any awards for best father."

My mother sighed. "I'm not going to defend him. All I can say was that he did his best."

"I'll do more than my best with my child. I want to be a good dad," I said with feeling.

"You can have both. A good relationship with your child and with your wife. Open up your heart just a little bit."

The doorbell rang and we both jumped as if we had been caught stealing. We were not a family given to emotional conversations or displays of feelings. It was uncomfortable for both of us but I was glad that we had had it. I'd never openly accused my father of being a less than adequate father in front of my mother.

Hearing her say that she was not going to defend him was evidence that I'd been right. He had spent too much time at work and neglected me as his son.

I followed my mother to the door. She flashed me a reassuring smile and opened the door. Maria stepped in and she and my mother kissed each other on the cheek. When it was my turn, I enfolded her in my arms and held her tight. She felt so good and so soft.

He sisters trailed after her followed by her parents. We exchanged greetings and then stood in a circle as I did the introductions.

"You're most welcome to our home," my mother said, leading the way into the living room.

Maria and I sat next to each other on the couch and I revisited the urge to take her hand into mine. Two maids came into the living room carrying trays bearing drinks.

Almost everyone except for Maria accepted a glass of white wine and afterwards, when the maids left, my mother steered the conversation, something she was very good at.

"I can't tell you how happy I am that Maria is going to be part of our family," she said, favoring Maria with a warm smile. "She'll agree with me that we bonded from the very first time we met."

A huge smile covered Mrs. Swan's face. "That is wonderful to hear. We think that Stephen is a wonderful young man and we know that they'll be very happy together."

"The only thing that concerns us is the fact that they've known each other for such a short time," Mr. Swan said, surprising all of us who were familiar with his quiet ways.

"We already talked about that dad," Maria said.

"Still, I think it's a valid concern but I don't think it's up to us to stand in their way. We can only encourage them in their marriage."

"I have friends who've gotten married after knowing each other for a decade, only to have them divorced after a few months of marriage," Amber said. "Sometimes it doesn't really matter how long two people have known each other for."

I was surprised and grateful for her support. "Maria and I are expecting a child," I said. "We both want to provide a stable home for our child and we'll do everything in our power to ensure that we do."

"Very well," Mr. Swan said.

"Stephen and I are going to cover the cost of the wedding of course," my mother said.

"How big a wedding are you thinking of?" Mrs. Swan asked.

"A small wedding," Maria said. "Just family and friends."

"We do have a lot of friends," my mother said.

There was good natured arguing from both sides but finally, we all agreed to cap it at two hundred people. We also settled on a date, a month from then.

Having gotten the difficult topics out of the way, dinner was a lively affair. My mother even got the quiet Mr. Swan to regale us with tales of his golfing.

"That was a successful evening, I'd say," I said to Maria as I drove us home.

I had an overnight bag with me as I was spending the night in her apartment. We'd taken to spending Friday nights at her place as she usually had an early shift at the bakery and then sleeping at my apartment on Saturdays.

"It was better than I'd hoped," Maria said. "I'm glad the wedding date and number of guests is out of the way. The only thing I have to decide now is who will be my bridesmaid."

"We agreed on one each, right?" I said. Jeremy was going to be my best man naturally.

"Yes," she said. "I'll ask Linda."

We reached Maria's apartment and after parking the car, we made our way in. I flicked on the lights and that's when I noticed that Maria looked tired. Worry came over me and I made a mental note to ensure that she took it easy. She had a child growing in her belly and needed as much rest as she could get and if I had anything to do with it, she was going to get plenty of rest.

MARIA

"You could have asked me to meet you at the bakery," Linda said as she slid into the bench opposite me. She eyed the greasy burger and fries in front of me with distaste.

I made a motion to indicate that my mouth was full of food and I couldn't respond.

"I can't believe you're eating that crap," she said and when the waitress came over, she ordered a salad and coffee.

"I used to say the same thing too," I said when I swallowed my food. "Until I got pregnant. I'll be honest, I've thought of nothing else all morning at work. This greasy burger and fries," I said.

Linda shook her head in amusement. "May it never happen to me."

"I hope it does, it's magical," I said and then told her about our first visit to the obstetrician and how special it had been to see our baby for the first time.

"Could you like see its head and body?" Linda said and I giggled recalling the little mass of darkness that Dr. White had said was our baby.

"Nope," I said and described to Linda what we'd seen.

"And that made you cry?" she asked incredulously.

I nodded and suddenly missed Amber. "Have you spoken to Amber recently?"

The waitress brought Linda's salad and coffee. She waited until we were along again before answering.

"Yesterday," Linda said. "She's still miserable but I tried to encourage her to shift her mind from the baby and make her dream of starting her own business come true."

My heart lurched. Now that I was pregnant with my own child, I could relate a little to how she had felt when she had learned that I was not going to carry her child. I hadn't planned on being pregnant for years but now that it had happened, the thought of suddenly not being pregnant filled me with sadness. The longing for a child was a deep-rooted need that could not be replaced by something else. But that something could help by distracting you.

"Jack told her that he was not in a rush to get a baby and had only gone along with it because he loves her and wants her to be happy. But he wanted them to wait and save up. I agree with him," Linda said.

"I feel so bad for her and I don't know how to reach out to her anymore," I said, misery coating my voice.

"How are the wedding preparations going? Is Mrs. Cohen a nightmare? I've heard mothers-in-law are?" Linda said.

"I've left it all to her capable hands and she's awesome. She's arranged for us to meet the wedding planner on Saturday but it's more of an update than hashing out stuff," I said, relieved that I had to do very little.

"Isn't it nice to be rich?" Linda said.

"I suppose so but it's also more like Creamy Creations is smack in the middle of that industry and she's made loads of connections over the years," I said.

"Still, it's nice that you don't have to think about a budget or deal with the financial worries other couples deal with," Linda said.

"Yes, of course," I said and beamed. "I also enjoyed the trip to Paris."

"I need to find me a millionaire," Linda declared which made me laugh as she was the least materialistic person I knew.

"I hate to imagine the amount of money he spent that weekend alone," I said.

"Don't worry about that. A weekend to Paris is not going to dent Mr. Money's bank account."

"That's what he said, but it feels so wrong," I said. "And please don't call him that. His money does not define him."

"Relax," she said. "Don't get your panties in a twist. I was kidding and I like him. I think he's a pretty nice guy, all things considered."

"I'm glad to hear that because I came to ask you to be my Maid of Honor," I said. "Look what you made me do!"

"What?" Linda said.

"I had a nice little speech planned out about what a good sister you are to me and how much I love you."

Linda waved a hand away. "I know all that and I don't need to hear it."

"So, will you?" I said.

She held my gaze. "I'd love to be your Maid of Honor but there's one thing I'd love more than that."

"Go on," I said wondering what she was cooking up in her unpredictable mind.

"What would make me really happy was if my sisters whom I love so much would bury the hatchet and we could go back to our three lane friendship," Linda said. "And I have an idea on how to make it happen."

"I'm listening," I said.

"Ask Amber to be your Matron of Honor," she said. "She'll be honored and touched that you asked her."

"But what about you?" I wasn't too sure about asking Amber to be my Matron of Honor although I could see Linda's point.

"I'll be happy to mingle with the guests. Actually, I'll be looking forward to it. Might find myself a single man in the process."

The prospect of asking Amber to be my Matron of Honor filled me with horror. "What if she says no?"

Linda shrugged. "Then you'll know you tried and you have another maid of honor ready to step into her shoes. Come on you can do it."

"Okay."

"Good, pass by the salon. I know for a fact that she's working this afternoon," Linda said.

"My, you're pushy," I said.

"If you wait, you'll lose your nerve," she said.

"I don't have it anyway," I said. I wasn't averse to asking Amber to be my Matron of Honor, I just didn't want my offer to be rejected. Amber held on to her anger more than most people and this time, it was something that she had wanted very much.

"I would offer to take you but I have to go back to work," Linda said.

"It's okay, I'll go alone." I inhaled deeply. "I promise," I added when she stared at me pointedly.

Butterflies fluttered in my stomach, refusing to ease up even when I said goodbye to Linda and took a cab to the beauty salon where Amber worked. The lunch time crowd had thinned out when I got there but Amber was working on a client.

She looked up from her client's head and saw my reflection in the mirror. Her first reaction was a tentative smile which stilled the butterflies still fluttering in my belly.

"Hi," I said.

"Hi. What are you doing here?" she said.

"I came to see you briefly."

She glanced at her client. "I'm a little busy as you can see."

"I know but I won't be long and you don't have to stop what you're doing." I couldn't believe how nervous I was and yet I was speaking to my sister.

"Okay," she said.

I quelched the nausea rising up my throat. The worst she could do was say no and if she did, Linda would step in. But it was more than that. It wasn't just about becoming my matron of honor. It was about our relationship as sisters. I didn't want to lose that.

"I came to ask you to be my Matron of Honor," I said, staring intently at her.

Amber's mouth fell open and she stopped what she was doing and just gaped at me. "You want me to be your Matron of Honor after everything that's happened between us?"

"You're my sister. That will never change," I said. "As for what happened it was not your fault or mine. It just happened."

She went back to her work, dashing my hopes. Instead of diving in and trying to convince her, I left her side and strolled to the reception area of the salon, to give her time to think.

I fished out my phone and found a message from Stephen.

Stephen: Hey babe, how did lunch with Linda go? Did she say yes?

Me: It was interesting and no she did not say yes. She suggested that I ask Amber as a way to heal the rift between us.

Stephen: A good idea. Did you ask her?

Me: I'm at her work place now. I asked her and now she's thinking about it. I'm as nervous as I was when we were waiting to see Dr. White.

Stephen: That's nervous indeed. The worst-case scenario?

Me: She says no. Linda said if she says no, she'll be the Matron of Honor no problem.

Stephen: But it's about your relationship as well.

I loved how Stephen got things so fast.

Me: Yes.

Stephen: All the best. Tell me what she says.

I checked and responded to my emails and the next time I checked my watch, half an hour had gone by. Just when I was about to give up, Amber walked into the reception area with her client and walked her to the door. Then she came to where I was sitting.

"Do you want to go for coffee next door?" she said, staring at me warily.

"Make it tea and you have yourself a deal," I said and jumped to my feet.

We left the salon and went to the café next door. I felt guilty because I should have been at work catching up on my admin tasks. But sorting my issues with Amber was important too, I said to myself.

We ordered tea and coffee and sat studying each other for a few seconds without talking.

"What brought this on?" Amber finally said. "If I were you, I'd not ask me to be the Matron of Honor."

I shrugged. "It has to be one of my sisters because you're both my best friends." Unexpected tears sprouted into my eyes.

The reserved façade she had worn melted and she leaned forward and placed her hand over mine. "Don't cry and you two are my best friends too." Then it was her turn to tear up.

She wiped off the tears impatiently with the back of her hand. "I'm sorry, I've been such an asshole. I couldn't get out of my own self-pity and be happy for you. Don't think that I'm not thankful for the sacrifice you were ready to make for Jack and me."

"I would do anything for you," I said, my voice catching.

"Me too," Amber said. "I'm sorry about my behavior the last couple of weeks. I'm deeply ashamed of myself. Forgive me?"

Relief surged through me. "Done! Does this mean that you'll be my Matron of Honor?"

"Absolutely," Amber said. "I would love to."

I took her hands in mine and smiled at her. "You have no idea how happy that makes me. Thank you."

She smiled. "You're welcome." A pensive expression came over her features. "How's the baby?"

"Good. I think it's going to be a girl but Stephen is betting on a boy," I said, conflicted as to what to say and what not to say.

She laughed. "I'm with Stephen. I'm betting on a boy."

"We went for our first obstetrician's visit," I said and just like I'd shared with Linda, I told her about the scan.

Amber laughed until she cried. "I'd have loved to see that blob. I bet I would have cried too."

"It'll happen for you one day," I said.

"I know. I believe that now. Meanwhile, I'm thinking of starting my business. Jack and I have enough savings and he wants me too."

"I think that's a great idea. Let me know if there's anything you need my help with," I said.

"I will," Amber said. "By the way, what color of dress am I going to wear?"

"Whatever you want," I said. "I'm going to try on a few dresses next week. Want to come? It'll give you a chance to look at dresses as well."

"I would love to. Choosing wedding gowns is my absolute favorite thing to do," Amber said enthusiastically.

STEPHEN

The wedding planner's office was a walking distance from Maria's bakery and we opted to walk while enjoying the nice afternoon weather. I kept Maria's hand in mine as we strolled down the street. It felt good to be a regular guy walking down the street with his woman, instead of Stephen, the Cohen heir.

I had another surprise that I was cooking up for Maria. One that would ease up her work load at the bakery considerably and I knew she was going to love it.

When we stepped into the wedding planner's office, we were shown into the conference room where we found my mother already there seated with a dark-haired woman, whom I assumed to be the wedding planner.

I knew a lot of wedding planners too but I'd never met her.

"Marjorie, this is my son Stephen and his fiancée, Maria Swan," my mother said.

We all shook hands.

"We've spoken on the phone," she said to Maria.

"Yes, we have," Maria said. "It's a pleasure to meet you in person."

"Please have a seat," Marjorie said, and opened one of the color folders she had in front of her. "I know you're both busy people so we'll dive straight into business."

A soft knock came on the door and a woman brought in a tray with chilled water and glasses, which she proceeded to serve us. Meanwhile Marjorie snapped open her laptop and waited for the woman to pour water in glasses.

"So let's start with the basics. What colors are you thinking of, ideally two or three?"

I glanced at Maria, completely lost.

"I should know this since I'm a baker but I can't think of the two colors I want," Maria said helplessly. She turned to me.

"Black and white?" I offered.

The three women looked at me as if I'd lost my mind. I questioned my decision to meet with the wedding planner with Maria. Clearly not my forte. It was one thing to socialize with them in conferences and talk cakes but weddings and themes...I was lost.

"No pressure," Marjorie said smoothly. "Let me show you a few combinations and see if any catches your eye."

For the next few minutes, she showed us combinations of colors until they all started to look the same. I could see the same look of frustration on Maria's face. She was getting too exhausted from her early mornings at work. I felt pleased with myself that I'd sorted that particular problem.

Maria finally pointed to a combination of Peach and gold.

Next was the meal, sit down or buffet? The questions were endless and an hour later, I could tell that Maria had reached the end of her rope.

"Are we done here?" I said in a tone that left Marjorie with no choice but to say that we were done.

She and my mother exchanged a look.

"We have enough," Marjorie said.

I stood up and helped Maria to her feet. We thanked Marjorie and my mother and made our escape.

"I don't know what's wrong with me," Maria said as we walked back to the bakery. "I think my brain is turning to mush. I became overwhelmed and I couldn't wait to leave."

"Hey, if it's any consolation, I felt overwhelmed too," I said.

"Will you come by later," she said when we reached the bakery.

I leaned in to kiss her. "I'll be there."

It was on the tip of my tongue to tell her that I loved her and then I caught myself. I was confusing affection and love. What I felt for Maria was fondness. I liked her as a friend and she was someone whose company I enjoyed.

Love did not figure in that equation. I took a cab back to the office and found that Ryan was already in my office. He stood up when I entered the reception area and we shook hands.

"Come in," I said, gesturing towards my office.

I closed the door after he entered and went to sit behind my desk. Ryan was a baker in one of our franchises and had left to join his wife in the cafe she had started. He had worked there for a full year but had called me recently to tell me that he was loving it less and less.

He missed working in a bakery and had asked me to tell him if something came up. Seeing how tired Maria was getting, I'd immediately thought of Ryan. Today proved that I'd been right in asking him to come in for a chat.

"Maria Swan is the bakery owner I was telling you about," I said and gave him some information about Maria and the bakery.

Ryan was interested and willing to start immediately. The good thing with him was that he required no training and he knew all our products.

"Shouldn't I meet her first," Ryan said. "Be sure that we are a good fit?"

I waved his concerns away. "You will be. I've not told you this but she's also my fiancée. She needs the help even though she doesn't see it right now."

"Okay then. I'll be happy to start tomorrow and the early morning shifts are a breeze for me," Ryan said.

We agreed that he would do the paper work later the following day with Maria. That evening, when I left work, I felt inordinately pleased with myself and I couldn't wait to tell Maria about it. But like a sweet dessert, I would save it until later.

～

"How did the rest of your afternoon go?" Maria asked me as she diced the vegetables for stir-fried rice.

"Good," I said. "I got a lot done. And you?"

"Busy," Maria said. "We got an avalanche of custom orders this afternoon. It's making my head spin to see just how fast we are growing. I'm giving your idea of hiring another baker some serious thought," she said.

I kept my thoughts to myself but congratulated myself internally. We talked about the visit to the wedding planner again and agreed that it hadn't been our finest hour. I was glad that we could laugh about it.

We ate dinner in the kitchen when it was ready and as I cleaned up, Maria went to take a quick shower before bed. I finished with the kitchen and followed her.

"You look so enticing in there but I'll take a shower first," I said and headed to the bathroom.

When I was done, I returned to Maria's bedroom with a towel draped around my waist.

"A walking temptation," Maria said.

"You are the temptation," I said, pulling away the towel and flinging it over the chair.

I slipped into the sheets and immediately pulled her to me, pleased that she wasn't wearing anything. "Just the way I like you."

"This feels so good," she said laying her head on my chest.

I stroked her soft, silky back, letting my fingers drop to her curvy ass. I was aroused as hell but there was no rush. We had the whole night. Maria raised her head and moved up to kiss me on the mouth. I stroked tendrils of her hair and tucked them behind her ear.

"How did I get so lucky?" I said, when she drew back to stare into my eyes.

"I'm the lucky one," she said and brushed her lips against mine.

We kissed softly at first and then the kiss grew more heated. She tasted of peppermint and smelled fresh and clean. I teased her nipples with my thumbs and she moaned softly, letting me know how good she was feeling.

Maria placed her hand behind my head and pushed me down to suck her nipples.

"I love a woman who isn't shy about saying what she wants," I said.

"I want you too much to be shy," she said as I took a nipple into my mouth and swirled my tongue around it.

Maria squealed and trembled. "That feels too good," she cried.

I paused what I was doing. "There is no such thing as too good."

"Please don't stop," Maria said.

I held both of her breasts in my hands and pressed them together. I licked her nipples in turns and then shifted my attention to her belly, planting kisses on her bare skin.

As we were leaving Dr. White's office, there had been a woman waiting to see the doctor with a belly so big, I was sure she was close to giving birth. I couldn't wait to see Maria like that. She was going to be so beautiful.

I moved between her legs and gently spread them apart. Her arousal scents teased my nostrils and I let out a growl as I lowered my head until I was between her legs, and teased her clit with my tongue.

In the last few weeks, Maria had become more responsive than usual and I loved how tightly she gripped my head and squeezed me with her thighs. I licked and teased until she was close the coming.

I pushed her knees up, gripped my cock and wedged myself between her thighs. I teased her entrance before pushing my cock into her dripping pussy. I closed my eyes as I plunged deep into her heated core.

"Fuck Maria," I said.

Sex with Maria was the best I'd ever had. No woman had ever affected me the way she did, both emotionally and physically. She arched her hips and met me thrust for thrust. I rode her like a beast forgetting the warning to myself to be gentle with her.

Not that she wanted gentle.

"Harder Stephen," she cried. "Faster. Oh God, yes."

How was I supposed to control myself when she said such things? I plowed into her and she dug her fingers into my shoulders. Then she cried out as her pussy walls clenched my cock, driving me to my release.

"That was great," Maria said when our breaths returned to normal. She let out a long, drawn-out yawn. "I wish I didn't have to go to work so early in the morning."

That was my cue to tell her my surprise. I couldn't wait to see her reaction. Not wanting to miss anything, I propped my head up with my elbow so that I could watch her.

"You won't, after today," I said.

"Oh why is that?" she said.

My pulse quickened. "I hired a new baker for you. His name is Ryan and he's worked in one of our bakeries for many years. He knows all our products and needs no training."

Maria stared at me without speaking, probably digesting what I had just told her. Good bakers were difficult to find and she knew that. I brushed hair away from her face.

"He and his wife run a cafe but he told me a couple of weeks ago that he missed the atmosphere of the bakery. I thought of him when I saw how tired you were becoming and luckily, he said yes."

I waited for the gush of gratitude but none was forthcoming. Maria slowly and deliberately sat up in bed. "You hired someone for my bakery without asking me?" she said.

The twitch in her mouth warned me that all was not well.

"You need more help in the bakery," I pointed out, swinging my legs over the edge of the bed to sit up.

Maria jumped to her feet and pulled the sheet from the bed which she wrapped around herself. She paced up and down the room, clearly pissed off.

I reached for my boxer briefs and pulled them on. "I thought you'd be happy."

She turned to me. "What you're doing Stephen is controlling my life. I'm still trying to wrap my head around the fact that you actually went and hired someone behind my back."

"I wanted to surprise you."

"I'm too angry to deal with this right now. Please leave."

My jaw fell. "You're throwing me out of your house?"

Instead of responding, she glared at me and stalked out of the room. I hurriedly put on my clothes and went after her. She was at the front door holding it open.

MARIA

I was still fuming the following morning when I woke up. The events of the previous night played in my head. When Stephen had realized that I meant it when I asked him to leave, he had left without another word.

What he did was unforgiveable. My sisters and I had discussed controlling men and how it all begins. Stephen and I aren't even married yet. How would he be when we got married? Was I making a huge mistake agreeing to marry him for the sake of our baby?

But I wasn't just marrying him because of the baby. I'd never been drawn to another man as I was to Stephen. I'd been looking forward to getting married to him but now I wasn't so sure. Was he revealing his true colors?

Conflicted, I got up and went into the shower. I was glad that I had work to occupy me and then later in the afternoon, I was meeting my sisters, my mother and Mrs. Swan in a bridal store owned by one of her friends.

I finished showering, dressed and headed downstairs to the bakery. As I was opening the back door, I heard a sound behind me, like that of someone clearing their throat. The hairs at the back of my neck rose and my heart rate went up.

I'd never heard of an incident since I moved upstairs and the streets were pretty quiet at this time of the morning. My mind worked fast. How the hell was I going to protect myself and my child? My hands instinctively went to my belly, then I spun around.

"Hi," a blond-haired man said, standing a few feet away from me. "I'm sorry I scared you, I thought you'd see me but obviously you didn't."

"Who are you?" I said, my hands damp with sweat.

"I'm Ryan Smith. Stephen said he'd tell you to expect me this morning."

I cursed Stephen again internally. He had not only hired someone without asking me, he had also told him to come into work. Fresh anger gripped me. I considered my options. I could tell Ryan there had been a mistake and to go back home.

But that would be so unfair and it hadn't been his fault. This was all Stephen's fault. I let out a sigh and went to him.

"It's nice to meet you. My name is Maria Swan." We shook hands.

"It's a pleasure," he said.

He had a friendly face and when I met his gaze, I felt instantly comfortable with him.

"I can open the door if you like," he said and I gave him the key.

He opened the door and held it for me. Inside, I followed my usual routine, turning on the lights and washing my hands to start working on the morning's baking.

Ryan mimicked my actions and helped me carry flour and the other ingredients we needed for the pastries, cakes and muffins. There was no doubt that Ryan knew his way around a kitchen and as Stephen said, he didn't need any training.

He took over the cakes and I concentrated on the muffins.

"Stephen told me that you and your wife run a cafe?" I said to him as we worked side by side.

"Yes, we do," he said looking up with a smile. "We do very little baking and as I told Stephen, I miss it. I found myself at the office a lot of the times and when I was in the kitchen, I was getting in her way. She's a chef. Maybe one day we'll add baked products to our menu."

Later, while I oversaw the deliveries, he continued working in the kitchen and I grudgingly admitted that Stephen may have been right.

The way in which he did it was the problem. Peter was due in later in the afternoon but everyone came in and I introduced them to Ryan.

Peter came in at one o'clock and the two men took to each other which was important as they would be working together. We went to the office for me to input his information into our system.

It turned out that he preferred the morning shift, which left him free in the afternoons to help out at the café.

"My creative well will have been filled and I can go and do the admin stuff," Ryan said.

"I understand that perfectly well. Baking keeps me sane," I said. "It would drive me crazy if the only thing I had to do was office work."

"That's exactly how it was for me. I was grumpy as hell and I'm sure I was driving my wife crazy. She'll thank you for giving me a job doing what I love."

Afterwards, I gave him the key and we agreed that he would open the bakery on Monday. I wasn't worried since he had Stephen's vouch of trust. I hurried to my apartment upstairs, took a quick shower. I then dressed in a dress that would be easy to remove since I'd be spending the afternoon trying on wedding gowns.

I arrived at the bridal boutique a few minutes late. My first thought when I saw it was that I couldn't possibly afford the wedding gowns there. It was one of those stores that reeked of wealth and class. Then I remembered that Mrs. Cohen had offered to buy the gown.

I'd been adamant that I'd buy my own gown but so had she. Stephen had urged me to accept the gift and eventually, I grudgingly had.

I paused to admire the stunning silky wedding gown in the display window. I made my way in and was met with racks of wedding gowns and quite a number of people shopping.

"Maria," my sister Amber called, beckoning me over.

We hugged and kissed and then she took my hand and led me out of the floor of the store to one of the rooms off a hallway.

"We get to have a private room," Amber said. "I could get used to hobnobbing with these rich folk!"

I laughed. "Hobnobbing."

What Amber had called a room was more like a large comfortable living room.

"The bride is here!" my sister Linda said and stood up to hug me.

My mother and Mrs. Cohen hugged me too and after playing catch up, Mrs. Cohen's friend who owned the store came into the room with an assistant. They introduced themselves as Catherine and the assistant's name was Liz.

I felt like a fraud as I stood there while they took my measurements and questioned me on the style of wedding dress I preferred.

I couldn't tell them that weddings had never entered my mind. Less than two months earlier, I had no boyfriend and I hadn't been looking. If someone had told me then that I would be tying the knot in a couple of months, I would have laughed at their prediction.

"Can I just look at various styles," I said.

"Very smart," Catherine said. "We won't be long."

"What took you so long?" Amber whispered to me when Catherine and Liz left the room.

"You won't believe what Stephen did," I whispered back. "He hired a baker without asking me."

Instead of looking horrified as I thought she would, Amber giggled.

"Is he qualified?" she said.

"He's more than qualified. He's worked in the other franchises so he knows how to bake everything that we sell. That's not the point you know," I said irritably.

"I can't wait to see how you'll cope with married life. Married people are always doing things for each other without asking. It's sweet, I think."

"I don't," I snapped.

"I'm with Maria here," Linda said and I turned to check whether my mom and Mrs. Cohen were listening to our conversation.

They were engrossed in their own conversation.

"People should ask before doing such things. The bakery is Maria's after all," Linda said.

"It's different when you're married," Amber hissed back.

I rolled my eyes as they tossed argument after argument over me. It took me back to when we were kids. They could not go a full day without arguing or disagreeing over something.

Luckily, Catherine and Liz returned wheeling a long rack brimming with wedding gowns. My heart pounded hard as the looming wedding became more real.

"See if there's any that catch your eye," Catherine said. "We'll gather all the ones you like and you can try them on."

My feet felt like lead as I moved to the rack and started sifting through the gowns. I pulled out a gorgeous vintage silk-chiffon with beautiful embroidery on the bodice and another with a sweetheart neckline and a strapless bodice.

Soon I had six gowns that I wanted to try on. Excitement was creeping up on me and when the gowns I'd picked were taken to a fitting room, a lightness came over me. I felt like a princess as I wore the first gown, assisted by the shop attendant.

She zipped me up and when I stood in front of the mirror, tears filled my eyes. I looked so beautiful and I was going to marry Stephen soon. It wasn't how I'd envisioned my marriage to be but I was going to make the best of it.

I noticed the store attendant leave the fitting room, probably to give me a moment. My thoughts returned to my fiancé.

Stephen was an easy man to love and who knew, maybe with time, we would fall in love with each other. As it was, we were good friends and the chemistry between us could light a bonfire.

I'd never seen him with a child but from how caring he was with me, I suspected that he would make a wonderful father. Sadness came over me when I remembered the way we had parted ways. I had been so mad, I hadn't thought twice about kicking him out of my apartment.

Footsteps sounded behind me and at first, I thought it was the attendant who had returned. Instead, Linda entered and came to stand behind me.

"You look beautiful and sad," she said. "Are you okay?"

A sigh escaped my lips. "I was thinking about the fight that Stephen and I had."

"He was wrong to hire someone without asking you," Linda said. "But it's not an unforgiveable misdemeanor."

"It felt like it at the time," I said.

"Things always do at the time. I admire what you guys are doing and seeing you together, I could tell that you loved each other," Linda said.

"No, we don't love each other," I said.

She waved a dismissive hand. "I know what I saw. Just so you may know, Amber saw it too. We can't both be wrong," she said.

Love? I wanted to laugh out loud. What Stephen and I had was amazing chemistry. Definitely not love. Not on his part any way.

"I admire that and I hope to have that someday. Forgive him and move on. Enjoy your time together and your wedding. These other things are just blots in the landscape," Linda said.

STEPHEN

We were closing on an investment the following Monday and I was reviewing the deal documents once again. You could never be too careful. My office phone rang and I lifted it from the cradle. My secretary didn't come in on Saturdays and I'd directed the calls to my office.

"Hello," I said and smiled when Ryan's voice sounded from the other side.

"Hi," he said cheerfully. "I just thought I'd let you know how the day went."

"Yes, I'd love to hear," I said.

He recounted how he had gotten to the bakery before Maria got there and was apologetic because he had frightened her. She'd been great about it though and welcomed him to the bakery.

My smile grew wider as he spoke. Relief surged through me that Maria had not given him marching orders.

"She's a wonderful boss and I like everyone else who works there. Thanks for hooking me up, Stephen," he said.

"You're welcome."

An avalanche of longing for Maria came over me. We'd never gone this long without communicating. A picture formed in my mind of the last time I'd seen her. She'd been consumed by barely controlled rage. I'd never seen her so angry.

But despite all that, she had been kind and welcoming to Ryan. My heart constricted with a strong emotion I couldn't define, coupled with admiration. She'd not let our fight dictate how she treated Ryan.

She had given him a chance and in doing so, she had gained an invaluable member onto her team. Not that that justified my behavior. It did not. I'd had a lot of time to think and what I did had bordered on behaving in a controlling manner.

I'd crossed the boundaries of acceptable behavior. I had put myself in Maria's shoes and reversed our roles. I cringed as I imagined how upset I would be if she hired someone on my behalf without discussing it with me.

I don't know what I could have been thinking when I made that decision to call Ryan. I had to make things right between us. The only way to do that was to apologize in person.

My cell phone rang, interrupting my thoughts. The call was from the VP of a tech company we had invested in years earlier. George and I had grown from business acquaintances to good friends and we spent the next half hour on the phone chatting.

Afterwards, I kept glancing at my phone. Maria had gone wedding gown shopping and I assumed it was an exercise that would take all of the afternoon. I stayed in the office until six in the evening when I was sure that she would be back home.

I got my driver to drop me off at her apartment and then dismissed him for the rest of the weekend. I had no plan except to apologize. Heart pounding, I hit the buzzer and waited. No response. I hit it again.

When there was no answer, I knew that she wasn't home. The buzzer made a deafening sound that you could not ignore. I stood there as frustration grew inside me. Where could she have gone to? Maybe for coffee or dinner with her sisters.

I hung around for another twenty minutes. I finally gave up and flagged down a cab to drive me home. Misery came over me at the thought of spending another evening without Maria. I missed her and would do anything to make things right between us.

I got home and rode the elevator to my apartment. Upon entering, I shut the door and when I looked up, I saw her, seated on the couch just looking at me. I blinked several times, sure that I'd missed her so much I was now losing my mind.

"Maria?" I said closing the distance between us.

"I hope you don't mind that I used the spare key you gave me," she said.

I'd given her the key when I had to leave early one morning and I wanted her to sleep in. "That's why I gave it to you."

I went and sat on the far end of the couch. "I'm glad you came. I was at your place. I waited for twenty minutes, gave up and came home."

"Oh," Maria said, staring at me incredulously.

I inched closer and took her hand. "I wanted to apologize. I behaved like a pompous, know it all ass."

She cracked a smile. "That just about sums it up."

"I shouldn't have hired Ryan. It was not my place. I should have recommended him and left the rest to you," I said. "I'm sorry and it won't happen again."

"I'm sorry too," Maria said. "I shouldn't have overreacted."

"You mean kicked me out of your apartment?" I teased.

She giggled. "I've never kicked anybody out of my apartment. I let my anger get out of control."

My heart swelled until if felt as if it would burst. "I'll try not to make you angry again."

"Ryan was great," she said. "He fit in perfectly as if he's been working with us for years."

"I'm glad," I said. "How did the wedding gown shopping go?"

"Perfectly. I got the dress," she said. "I can't wait for you to see it."

I inched closer, wanting, no needing to have her in my arms. "Can I hold and kiss you?"

"Yes," she murmured.

"Sit on me," I said and she got up and sat on my lap.

I wrapped one hand around her waist and let the other one rest on her belly. I raised my head and she brought her head down to kiss me. The moment our lips met, I felt as if I'd come home. She tasted of spring and summer.

I captured her bottom lip between mine and nibbled on it. Maria groaned and let me know with her hands and her body that she had missed being with me. She raked her fingers through my hair and molded my shoulders with her hand.

My hands left her waist to roam over her body finally moving to her breasts to cup them. Her nipples did not disappoint and were already hard and pointed. She let out soft cries when I rubbed my thumbs over them.

I lost track of time as we made out on the couch. Breathing heavily, I broke the kiss and stood up. Maria wrapped her legs around my waist and I carried her to my bedroom.

She planted soft, teasing kisses on my neck and pushed her nipples against my chest. I couldn't wait to have her naked and in my arms. I lay her on the bed and slowly undressed her, kissing her bare skin when the need to touch her got too much.

Then she was gloriously, sexily naked and good enough to eat. I undid the buttons of my shirt and pulled own my pants. Maria giggled at the sight of my tented boxer briefs.

"You look so hot like that," she said.

"Should I keep it on?" I said and cupped my arousal through my boxer briefs.

"Remove them," Maria said in an affected voice.

I hauled them down and joined her on the bed. "I've missed you so much," I said and pulled her on top of me. "I don't want to hurt the baby."

"I love how careful you are," Maria said, her body draped over mine.

I stroked her back and curvy ass, pulling her against my erection. Our lips found each other and we kissed deeply, filling the room with noises of our pleasure.

We made slow, leisurely love and when it was over, Maria lay spent on top of me.

"I love sex with you," she said.

I squeezed her. "I love sex with you too."

Her belly grumbled.

"So does your stomach," I said and we both laughed. "There's some food in the fridge. Let's go warm it up."

"You're a keeper," Maria said and slid off me. She padded into the walk-in closet and returned minutes later wearing one of my t-shirts and another draped across her hand. "There you go." She tossed it to me on the bed.

I got up and wore my briefs as well as the t-shirt. We walked to the kitchen hand in hand and foraged for leftovers in the fridge. There was pasta and meatballs as well as a coleslaw salad.

After warming the food, we sat at the island eating and sipping on water.

"What are we doing tomorrow?" Maria asked.

"What about our driving lesson?" I said.

"Okay, scary but okay," Maria said.

"There's no reason to be scared. I'll go very slowly." I leaned across to remove a small piece of pasta on the side of her lip. I took the opportunity to brush her lips with my finger. "They're swollen."

"That's because of how much kissing we've done," Maria said.

"And yet, it's not nearly enough."

She widened her eyes as if the very idea was shocking to her. I laughed. We chatted as we ate dinner and afterwards, we cleaned up and returned to the bedroom.

I pulled out a remote from the dresser drawer and pressed a button. The wall slid down to reveal a hidden TV screen that occupied the whole space. "Want to watch a movie?"

"Sure. I can't believe I'll be living here surrounded by all this fancy stuff," Maria said. "It can get intimidating you know."

"These are just material stuff. I've told you that before. They are there for us to enjoy but they can't replace human relationships."

I'd never once gotten an urge to cuddle up with a woman to watch a movie. I loved movies, back in the day when work didn't occupy so much of my time but relaxing with Maria made me make a decision to do it more often.

We settled on an old western classic and as we watched, my hand stole to her belly to caress it. Our baby was in there. I was going to be a dad. I couldn't wait for that day when I'd get to hold him or her in my arms.

"Do you feel any different now that you're pregnant?" I asked Maria.

"A lot different. I feel sleepy in the afternoons and I never used to feel sleepy during the day. Oh and I'm definitely a lot more emotional. I saw myself in a wedding gown and cried," Maria said. "How weird is that?"

"It doesn't sound weird to me. I would have cried if I'd seen you in a wedding gown."

"You know that's not what I mean," she said and punched me playfully.

We talked more than we watched the movie but it was fine since we'd both watched it before and in Maria's case, multiple times.

"Have you ever taught anyone how to drive?" Maria asked me.

"No, but it's not rocket science," I said. "But I was taught and I remember how that went."

"Was it a good experience?" she asked.

"It was okay," I said. Learning anything when you were young was always easier that learning as an adult but I didn't tell Maria that. No use adding to her anxiety. "How come you've never been interested in learning how to drive?"

She went tense and I reacted instinctively and massaged her shoulders.

"We were in an accident once and the experience haunted me for a long time. I associated driving with accidents and still do, actually, though the fear is fading now."

I knew what trauma did to a person's brain. It made you freeze. "I think you're very brave to do it."

She gave a nervous laugh. "Let's see how brave I'll be tomorrow. It's easy to be, lying here in your arms."

"I'll be right there next to you and you'll be just fine."

MARIA

I woke up at my usual hour with a pounding heart. I looked about me in confusion until I knew where I was. Beside me, Stephen was sleeping peacefully, his features relaxed and absolutely still. Even after my surroundings made sense, my heart was still pounding.

It didn't take long to figure out what the problem. The driving lesson. I turned to my side and faced Stephen. The thought of being the one in the driver's seat filled me with terror. I'd tried several times to sit in the driver's seat in my sisters' cars and each time, I would sweat profusely.

I wanted to do well and overcome that fear of mine, but I was also afraid of letting Stephen down. I checked the time. Half past three in the morning. I got out of bed as quietly as I could and padded out of the bedroom to the kitchen.

I flicked on the kitchen lights and opened the fridge. I found some milk and poured myself a glass. I couldn't remember the last time I'd drank milk but since getting pregnant, I found myself wanting to drink or eat things that I'd never craved before.

I sat on the kitchen stool and took a swig. I made appreciative noises as the cold milk went down my throat.

"I wish I loved milk. That looks so tasty."

I jumped. I hadn't heard Stephen's footsteps. "What are you doing awake?" I said. "I hope I didn't wake you up."

He kissed my cheek and slid onto the stool next to mine. "No you didn't. I woke up to go to the bathroom and found you gone."

"I couldn't sleep," I admitted. "I woke up with a racing heart."

"Let me guess," Stephen said rubbing my back. "It's about the driving lesson."

"Yes. I'm such a baby."

"No, you're not. It's normal to be frightened of something that you've always been frightened of doing. If it makes you feel any better, today we'll do theory."

I turned to him with a raised eyebrow.

"I'll teach you what and where everything is and let you get a feel of the driver's seat but that will be it for today."

I exhaled. "Sounds good. I can do that." I slugged back the last of my milk.

Stephen took my glass and carried it to the sink. "Come on, let's go back to bed. I think you'll get some sleep."

I followed him obediently to the bedroom. Stephen got in after me and spooned me. It felt so good to have his hard body snuggling mine. I didn't fall asleep immediately but I wasn't as anxious as I had been and ten minutes later, my eyelids grew heavy and I gave in to sleep.

The next time I woke up, I was alone in bed. I stretched, glad that I'd gotten a few extra hours of sleep and took my time getting up to go to the bathroom to freshen up.

After washing my face and brushing my teeth, I straightened the bed and went in search of Stephen. In the hallway, tantalizing smells of something yummy frying wafted up my nostrils.

"Is that bacon I smell?" I said as I entered the kitchen.

"Right on time," Stephen said and turned off the stove.

I stood behind him and slipped my hands around his waist and rested my head on his back. "Good morning."

"Morning," he said and covered my hands with his. "I thought you might like some bacon."

I kissed his back and stepped back. "I'd love some bacon, thank you." I poured two cups of coffee from the coffee machine and carried them to the island.

Stephen followed with our breakfast, two plates piled high with bacon and scrambled eggs. He set them on the island. "Did you manage to get some sleep?"

I nodded.

He bent down and kissed my belly. "Good morning baby."

My heart melted and tears sprung to my eyes. It was becoming more and more real. Stephen and I were going to become parents. It's an odd feeling to love my baby so much and yet I haven't seen him or her.

I gobbled up my breakfast and then Stephen and I got ready for my first driving lesson.

In the basement parking garage, Stephen led me to a gorgeous blue car, a cute compact, brand-new BMW. I ran my fingers over the shiny exterior. "Nice, I didn't know you drove a BMW as well."

"I don't," Stephen said. "It's yours."

I went absolutely still and shifted my gaze from the car to Stephen. "What do you mean it's my car?" I asked in a shaky voice.

"I bought it for you. Another surprise but I hope you'll love this one and accept it. It has cutting edge security features and I'll feel secure knowing that you and our baby are safe."

It was the mention of the baby that made it possible to play around with the idea that the gorgeous car in front of me could be mine. I admired it, conflict pulling me in multiple directions.

I wasn't averse to a beautiful car but what had I done to earn it? Everything I had in my life had been earned through hard work. My parents raised and educated us to be self-sufficient. The most expensive gift I'd ever been given by a man had been a necklace and it hadn't been that expensive either.

Stephen unlocked the car and came around to open the passenger door. I get in and inhale the sweet scent of leather and crisp newness. The seats are cream in color and the rest of it is shiny black.

Stephen gets into the driver's seat and turns to me. "What do you think?"

"It's beautiful," I said, my voice filled with awe. I swallowed hard as he turned the ignition and the engine roared to life.

As he eased out of the basement parking garage, I imagined myself in Stephen's seat driving and instead of a sweat breaking out of my skin, my heart pounded with excitement and anticipation.

"Where is this field, we're going to?" I said.

"About fifteen minutes from here," Stephen said.

I settled back in my comfortable seat and stared at the passing views. My mind was gloriously empty and it felt good to know that I had a long free day to spend with Stephen.

Traffic was light during the mid-morning and we got to the open field in the fifteen minutes that Stephen had predicted. My heart took on a faster pace when he brought the car to a stop and turned off the engine.

He turned to me and smiled. "There's absolutely no need to worry. No pressure whatsoever. You can even sit where you are if you like."

I beamed, soothed by his words. "That would kind of defeat the purpose of coming, wouldn't it?" I opened the door and got out.

Stephen and I met at the trunk and instead of getting out of each other's way, he pulled me into his arms and kissed me.

"I hope no one's watching us," I said when we paused for air. "We're too old to be making out in an open field."

"They can watch all they like," Stephen growled and kissed me again.

I relaxed into his arms and caressed the back of his neck. He smelled so good. All masculine. After a few minutes, we parted and I entered the driver's seat, while Stephen got into the passenger's seat.

"Have you ever sit in the driver's seat before?" he said.

I shook my head.

"Hold the steering wheel," he said. "How does it feel?"

I gripped the steering wheel and moved it from side to side. "It feels good." My hands trembled the slightest bit.

"I'll start by giving you a tour of the car," Stephen said and proceeded to point out everything to me.

Some I knew but some like the indicators, I didn't. Afterwards, I felt ready to turn on the ignition key. I jumped when the engine roared to life and then felt silly after. What had I expected it to do, purr?

Time flew by and before I knew it, it was lunch time and two hours had zipped by.

"That went great," Stephen said as we changed places. "What did you think?" he said when we entered the car.

"Exhilarated. I really think I can do this," I said, fired up.

"I'm glad you feel that way," Stephen said. "Next Sunday you'll get to move the car for the first time."

"I can't wait," I said and buckled my seatbelt.

"Let's look for a place to have lunch," Stephen said and drove out of the field and back to the road.

My stomach rumbled in response even though we'd had a late breakfast. "This little firecracker is making me really hungry these days," I muttered.

"Firecracker?" Stephen asked with a grin.

"Yes," I said. "That's what I call her privately. Sometimes I feel movement in my belly but logically, it's too early to be the baby. But I like to think that it is."

"I think it's the firecracker as well," Stephen said. "We're nearly there, hang on."

A minute later, he pulled onto a side road with a sign of a roadside café.

"I've been here before," Stephen said as we drove up to the parking lot. "They use produce from their own farms so everything is fresh and has that just harvested taste."

"Sounds nice," I said, my mouth watering already.

We chose an outdoors seating space that had a view of wooded hills. A nice breeze blew across my face and I closed my eyes and mind to everything but the coolness on my skin.

The server came with the menus and we ordered two bottles of water.

"What is looking good to you?" Stephen said as we scrutinized the menu.

"The chicken fettuccine with garlic sticks," I said. "Wait, the meatloaf and mashed potatoes looks good too."

"Let's do this, I'll get the meatloaf and mashed potatoes and

you get the chicken fettuccine and we'll share, okay?"
Stephen said.

"Good idea."

The server came by with our bottled water and took our
order for lunch.

"Do you come here often?" I said when the server withdrew.

"The last time I came here was almost two years ago with
Paige," Stephen said.

A burning sensation spread over my chest and I immediately
hated myself for it. How could I feel jealous over the fact that
Stephen and his ex-wife had done exactly what we were
doing? She had been his wife and they had shared their lives
together.

Of course Stephen had a lot of good memories of his
marriage. Plus, I had no right to feel jealous. Stephen and I
were not your conventional couple. We were getting married
to give our baby a safe, family environment to grow up in.

"It was a disaster," he said and chuckled.

"Why?" I said, intrigued.

"That's the day she started an attack on my capability of
being a good father," Stephen said casually. "She hit a raw
nerve, reminding me that I was my father's son. My father
had loved his work, probably more than he did his family
and by then I hadn't figured out that it was a choice he
made."

"Just like the choice you're making to be there for your child,"
I said.

"Exactly. We didn't talk for the next week," Stephen said.

The server came at that moment carrying our food. The delicious smell of grilled chicken filled the air.

"Enjoy your meal," she said and left.

"I could get full just by inhaling the smell," I said and Stephen laughed.

He kept laughing and proceeded to share the food, putting half of everything on each of our plates.

"Dig in," he said when he was done.

The food tasted better than it smelled. I ate quietly until the pangs of hunger dissipated.

"Can I ask you something?" I said. "Do you think that marriage is hard?"

Stephen didn't immediately answer my question. He gave it some thought for a few minutes, his brow creased in concentration.

"Marriage can be hard if you have expectations of each other and neither of you can meet them. Ours will work because we don't have romantic expectations of each other."

A slice of pain stabbed through my body. Stephen had spoken the truth but it still hurt.

STEPHEN

"I love how soft your skin is," I said to Maria as I rubbed the bath puff around her neck, scrubbing gently.

"Thank you," Maria said, standing still as I lathered the front of her body.

We had taken to taking a shower together every morning before we went to work since Ryan took all the morning shifts. Maria could go in later, which meant that I could drop her off. We spent most nights at my place though once or twice a week, we'd spend the night in her apartment.

"Your belly is becoming nicely rounded," I said, rubbing circles around her stomach.

"Our little firecracker is growing," Maria said and covered my hand with hers.

We shared a moment of quiet intimacy, our thoughts on our child growing in her belly. I continued washing her, scrubbing her arms and feet. I turned her around and did the same with her back before guiding her under the jets of warm water for a rinse.

Then it was her turn to wash me and I tried to stand as still as she had but my cock was letting me down. It jerked up and down, making Maria giggle. My laughter stopped abruptly when she stroked my cock, gripping it tightly as she moved her hand.

I groaned and rocked into her hand. She teased my balls with her other hand and they grew tight as she squeezed gently. Unable to keep my cool, I grabbed her and crashed her against my body.

She laughed and looped her hands around my neck and kissed me. I dropped my hands to her ass and pulled her against my erection. A need to take her in the bathroom came over me. I slipped a hand between her legs and stroked her pussy. Juices coated my fingers and hand.

I withdrew my hand after some moments and moved Maria to the wall. I lifted her and propped her against the wall. I kept one hand under her hips and with the other, I gripped my cock and pressed it into her pussy.

"Ohhhh," Maria screamed as I pushed my cock inside her

"Fuck," I said between clenched teeth. "You're unbelievably sweet."

"Deeper," Maria said when I paused, unsure whether I'd gone in too deep. With that angle, I penetrated her deeper than I ever had.

Water poured down my body as I pumped in and out and I wasn't sure whether it was the shower water or my sweat. I fucked her harder and faster, consumed by a primal need.

"I'm going to come," Maria cried, digging her nails into my shoulders.

"Come for me babe," I said and drove harder.

She breathed through her mouth making loud panting noises. A couple of minutes later, Maria's eyes rolled to the back of her head and she let out a loud, drawn-out cry. Her pussy throbbed and clenched around my cock and with a cry my release shot out of me, filling her with hot cum.

I kept pumping until I had gotten rid of every last drop. I found Maria grinning at me when my ability to focus returned.

"You look so sexy when you're coming," she said.

"Not sexier than you." I lowered her gently to the ground, took her in my arms and kissed her long and hard. "I'll never get enough of you."

"Me neither," Maria said, her smiling face upturned to me.

We rinsed off, dried and left the bathroom.

"Marjorie finalized with the venue yesterday," Maria said.

"That's a relief," I said, guilt flooding me because I hadn't been reading the emails that the wedding planner had been sending me.

"Yeah, she'll let us know when we're to go for a venue walk through," Maria said.

"Sounds good," I said.

After dressing, we headed to the kitchen for breakfast. I usually only had coffee as did Maria before she became pregnant but now, she had a craving for cereal.

"It's two and a half weeks to the wedding," Maria said, spooning cereal into her mouth.

"I can't wait to make it official," I said. "I have an idea. Why don't you move in with me? You will in two and a half weeks anyway."

A shadow of fear crossed her eyes.

"I don't know," she finally said. "It seems such a huge step."

"Bigger than getting married?" I teased, hoping to remove that worry from her beautiful face.

She grinned. "I guess not. Let me think about it, okay?"

"Sure, no pressure."

We finished breakfast and took the elevator down. My driver was waiting in the car and when he saw us, he jumped out and opened the back door for us. We dropped off Maria, and then he drove me to the office.

My calendar that day consisted of clearing my inbox. In some months, I got as many as five thousand emails and depending on my backlog, I sometimes dedicated a day to reading and responding to them.

The ones that get the first priority are from my team and they kept me occupied for the first two hours of the morning. We'd dipped our toes in practically every industry and there was always something going on that needed my attention or decision.

There were also emails from other VC's and I replied to most of these as well. Mid-morning, I got to the majority of the emails, which were from entrepreneurs seeking funding.

Most of them I only gave a cursory glance to, others I read a bit more but was the rare day when I got interested enough to put my team on a cold call email.

I had gone through at least twenty emails when one caught my attention. It was from three guys recently out of college. One of their friends' parents owned a restaurant and their biggest issue was deliveries. The bigger franchises did their own deliveries and had departments dedicated to that.

These guys had coded a delivery system and started a company called Delivery Magic and it had worked wonderfully well in their friend's parents' restaurant. Other restaurants were interested in using them but they needed funding.

They had attached a lot of documents from market research to projected growth to references. It was an impressive pitch and my pulse rate picked up as I went through the email again and the documents.

I couldn't remember the last time I'd been this excited about an idea. After I was done, I called Chris, a member of my team. He read the email and like me he got very excited. We called a couple of smaller establishments to ask about deliveries and most sounded exhausted by the very idea.

I liked their mission as well. To enable every establishment to deliver to the customer.

The office was a buzz of activity as we pulled in the other members of the team. We spent a fun afternoon in a buzz of excitement and wanting to go out and celebrate, I texted Maria and asked her if she wanted to go out for dinner that evening.

We received thousands of requests for funding and it was the rare day when we came across an idea that excited us. We spoke with the guys for Delivery Magic and asked them to come in the following day to present to us in person.

Chris and I had discussed going into it as shareholders, depending on how the discussions with the guys went and if they had approached other investors.

M aria had given me a key to her apartment and when I went to pick her up for dinner at half passed six, I used my key rather than ring the buzzer.

"I'm home," I teased stepping in.

There was no response. My footsteps echoed down the tiled floor. Then noises came from the bathroom down the hall-way, before the door swung open and Maria stepped out.

"Don't be startled," I said quickly. "It's me."

"Hi, when did you get here?" she said, the corners of her lips tugging up in an irresistible smile.

"Just now," I said and bent to kiss her when she got closer.

I followed her into her bedroom. Droplets of water sprinkled her back. In her bedroom, she unwrapped the towel and wiped the back of her neck.

"You missed a spot," I said but instead of taking the towel, I turned her around and licked the droplets off.

Maria moaned as I planted more kisses down her spine to the curve of her ass.

"You're lucky that we don't have time," I said, patting her ass regretfully.

"Tease," she said and dropped the towel on a chair. I sat at the edge of the bed and watched her getting ready.

"What are we celebrating?" Maria said.

"A sweet deal if it does go through," I said, not bothering with the details.

"What kind of a deal?" Maria said.

I explained to her about the guys who had emailed me and their current business model. My heart raced as I spoke about it.

"I haven't known you for years but I haven't seen you this excited about work before," Maria said, her head disappearing under a cream dress as she pulled it on.

"I have a gut feeling about this one," I said and stood to zip her up. "If it's as revolutionary as I and my team think it is, it can become one of our greatest scoops this year."

I explained it to her in further details, following her to the bathroom where she was combing her hair. She asked intelligent questions that didn't surprise me but I enjoyed myself.

When she was ready, we left and headed downstairs to my car. I'd made reservations at an Italian restaurant, a chic establishment that catered to a mixture of clientele, both young and mature.

Our table was ready and we were escorted straight there when I gave my name.

"May I take your drinks order as you relax?" the server said.

Maria asked for water and I did as well.

"You should have wine or beer if you like," she said.

"I'm fine with water," I said. I liked a glass or two of wine over dinner but since Maria found out that she was pregnant, I'd gone to drinking water like she was.

Wine was tastier when it was shared. He left the menus and we took our time perusing them. Maria decided on the lasagna and I ordered a steak, roasted potatoes and veggies.

When we were done choosing, I beckoned the waiter and we gave our order. Maria let out an odd sound from her throat that startled me and when I turned my gaze to her, I saw that she was stifling a giggle.

"What?" I said, smiling despite not knowing what was making her laugh.

"I was remembering the first time I saw you," she said. "I thought you were horrible and mean."

"Why?" I said, trying to recall the details of our first meeting. All I remembered was that seeing her had stolen my breath away and I had known that I wanted to see her again.

"You criticized the bakery," she said laughing.

"I apologize profusely," I said. "If I'd suspected that I was looking at the woman who would become my wife, I'd have behaved better. I'd worn my business cap that day but if it makes you feel better, I thought you were the most beautiful woman I had ever seen."

Maria cocked her head to the side and looked at me. "And now?"

"No, I don't think. I know it," I said.

MARIA

"**W**hat do you think of peach?" Amber said, holding a pretty dress against her body.

We had met after work to shop for Amber's matron of honor dress. She had shied away from picking a dress when I'd gotten mine, since Mrs. Cohen would have insisted on paying for it. We'd agreed to shop for her dress another time.

"I think it's meh," Linda said.

Amber put it back and continued going through the rack of bridesmaid's dresses. She found several she liked and draped them on her arm to try on later. We stayed for an hour helping Amber pick her dress. Afterwards, we went for coffee and to rest our legs before parting ways.

"How is the groom holding up?" Linda said sipping at her coffee.

A sigh escaped before I could stem it. Amber stopped what she was doing and looked at me questioningly.

"Trouble in paradise already?" Linda said.

"Shut up Linda," Amber said. "What is it honey? Wedding jitters?"

"No. Stephen asked me to move in with him," I said. I wasn't expecting gasps but I did expect a bit of surprise. I mean, the wedding was less than three weeks away and we could wait until then to move in together.

"So?" Linda said. "You're two are getting married anyway. It's not a bad idea to get used to living together before then."

"I'm with Linda there," Amber said. "It'll be fun and by the time you start living together, you'll have gotten used to it." She winked at me. "Plus you're already pregnant. We all know now that you aren't a virgin."

Ignoring that last sentence, I inhaled deeply. "I'm petrified by the idea honestly. What if we irritate the hell out of each other?"

"You will, after the honeymoon is over" Amber said. "But you'll soon get used to living together and enjoy it before the baby comes." A wistful look came over her features.

My heart squeezed knowing what was going through her mind. I chose not to say anything knowing it would make her feel worse.

"I guess you're right," I finally said.

"Have you spoken to Mom and Dad recently?" Linda asked me casually.

"No," I said and swallowed down guilty feelings. Prior to getting pregnant, I'd spoken to my mom every other day and visited them every week.

"Yeah," Linda continued. "That's what Mom said."

"I'll call and visit soon," I said, hoping that was the end of that but knowing Linda, there had to be a reason for mentioning it.

"What happened Maria?" Linda said. "Why the distance between you and the parents? Mom is sure that she must have said something that upset you."

The smart thing to do would have been to brush away mom's worries and reassure my sisters that all was well. But I was hormonal, there was a human being growing inside of me and my feet were tired from standing too much at the store. So I engaged my mouth before my brain. Always a mistake.

"Why would it upset me that Mom was more concerned with Amber's welfare than mine?" I blurted out.

Silence followed my words. My sisters stared at me open mouthed, probably shocked that I still harbored such bitterness. After the furor over my pregnancy had died down and I'd introduced my family to Stephen, the past events had started to play in my mind from the moment I agreed to carry Amber and Jack's baby.

The person who had stood out from the whole fiasco, apart from Amber of course, was my mother. I saw her pinched face as she waited for me to decide whether I was going to carry Amber's baby or not. Her joy when I said yes, but that was not a surprise, as any mother would be happy for her daughter.

It was how she reacted when Amber announced my pregnancy. She was pissed off at me and she had wanted me to give my baby to Amber and Jack to raise as their own, never mind that the baby was mine or even what I wanted. It had hurt. Deeply.

My way of dealing with it had been to stay away until the pain no longer ate at me. I'd almost reached there. If I hadn't opened my big mouth and blurted out the truth to my sisters.

"She wanted me to give my baby to Amber and Jack to raise as their own." Now that I had started, I couldn't seem to stop the flow.

"Maria, you know that's not how it went," Amber said, shock drawn on her pretty face.

"Tell me how it went then?" I dared her, knowing that I was right.

She opened her mouth to speak then closed it.

"Mom cared more about your happiness than mine. And she didn't care about the cost to me," I said hotly. "How do you think that felt?" I looked from Amber to Linda. A weary expression came over Amber's features.

I felt bad for bringing up a painful subject but it was the truth. No one had cared how it had affected me. Their concern had been Amber. I understood why but it had hurt and it still did that my own mother had thought it right that I should give my baby to my sister because she wanted a baby.

"I guess she thought she was doing the right thing?" Linda said, her tone unsure.

Amber placed her hand on mine. "I'm sorry Maria. I've had a lot of time to think about it and we were all wrong to put so much pressure on you. I was the worst and I guess mom was just following my cue. Forgive her. I know she regrets it now."

"How do you know?" I said, not willing to be placated.

"I just do," Amber said.

"You should have said no from the very beginning like I did," Linda said. "No is a complete sentence."

~

Talking to my sisters had given me the clarity of mind to make a decision on whether to move in with Stephen or not. Talking about the surrogacy issue had been painful but later that afternoon, I felt as if a weight had been taken off my shoulders.

Amber and I had cried together and then laughed. It felt as if our relationship was back to where it had been before she asked me to carry the baby for her. Back in my apartment, I took a walk around, trying to figure out what I'd miss and what I wouldn't. By the time I got to my bedroom, I was ready to start packing.

I pulled out suitcases from the closet and started emptying drawers. In the evening, I was still at it, and my back was beginning to hurt. I'd been working nonstop for a few hours, only stopping to answer Stephen's call. They were in a meeting with the guys from Delivery Magic and after ending my call, he was going to turn off his phone to avoid distractions.

I couldn't wait to surprise him the following day. On a whim, I decided to do it that evening. My heart pounded with excitement as I pictured Stephen's face if he found me at his apartment that night after work. He'd said they would probably order dinner and have it at the office, which meant I had a lot of time.

Marcus, one of Linda's friends owned a moving company and all of us used his services when we moved. I got him on the phone and told him what I needed. I was moving but not quite moving. I was only moving my clothes and stuff I needed with me. The rest was going to stay. I was glad that I was not parting with my apartment.

He squeezed me in later that evening and he came alone in a van. In less than twenty minutes, he had all my suitcases stashed in the van.

"You're moving up in the world," Marcus teased when I gave him my new home address.

Embarrassment came over me. The impostor feeling came back. It felt wrong to be moving into Stephen's posh apartment. Marcus teased me some more when he saw that there was a lobby attendant in the apartment.

The two men carried my suitcases to Stephen's apartment and then they left, leaving me alone. The apartment suddenly seemed even larger. Following my instructions, they had left my suitcases in the living room, and not wanting Stephen to find them there, I heaved them across the room, one a time.

There were six in total and luckily, the last two had wheels. I sat down on the bed when the last suitcase was safely in the closet. A sharp pain cut across my lower stomach then more cramps started in earnest.

My baby!

Panic swelled up inside me, threatening to swallow me belly-first. Something was going on inside my body and it wasn't good. I pushed myself to stand up and that's when I felt the wetness in my panties.

Fear curled itself around my heart. I couldn't stand it if I lost my baby. I'd read enough stories to know that a lot of women had lost their babies in early pregnancy. I pulled down my pants and peered at me panties. Red stains.

A scream filled the air before I realized that it had come from me. I was alone in the apartment and Stephen's cell phone was switched off. I inhaled deeply and refused to let the panic spreading in my chest go any further. I needed to think. Fast.

I needed to call for help. Frightened of making things worse, I painstakingly made my way to the living room where my purse was. Despite keeping my legs tightly squeezed together, they shook as I moved. My eyes filled with tears. I'd never been so frightened in my life. Every second felt like a lifetime as I made my way to the living room.

I fished my phone from my purse and called Linda. With a voice that was barely audible, I explained to her what had happened.

"I'm on my way," she said.

"Wait," I said. "You don't know the address." I rattled it off for her.

The next twenty minutes that it took for Linda to call me from the lobby were the longest in my life. I spoke to the lobby attendant and he allowed Linda to come up. To my relief, I saw that Amber was with her. They supported me from each side and as I explained we moved out of the house to the elevators.

"Everything will be just fine," Amber said. "Spotting is quite a common occurrence from what I've read. It doesn't mean anything ominous."

"I'm thinking it was those suitcases. Not the smartest thing you've ever done," Linda said.

"She doesn't need to hear that right now," Amber said.

I could hear their voices but what they were saying was not making sense. Nothing was. All I knew was that I was in an elevator and I needed to be in a hospital. Linda had parked her car illegally in front of the apartment building.

"Are you in pain?" Amber said sitting beside me in the back seat of the car.

I had to listen to my body to answer the question. "No pain."

"That's a good sign," she said. "Have you called Stephen?"

"He had a meeting that was going on until evening and we'd agreed to talk later tonight when it's over. He was having dinner in the office as well." My voice sounded the way I felt. As if I was going to burst into tears at any moment.

I bit my lower lip and wished that Stephen was with me. I longed for his calming presence. Amber draped an arm around me.

"It's going to be okay."

STEPHEN

"That's it for today," I told the group seated around the conference table.

"More like tonight," someone piped up and we all laughed. It was way after midnight, almost one o'clock. The meeting had gone on longer than I would have anticipated.

We were a full house with two representatives from our legal department, the three guys together with their legal representative as well and my team. We had spent the afternoon and evening hashing out details of the principle terms of the investment agreement. The boys had been resolute in selling a very small percentage of their shareholdings.

They wanted us to come in purely as silent investors with no or little input on how the company was run. We'd managed to put our foot down and reached an agreement that suited all of us. We were not done yet and there would be many more nights like the one we just had.

I popped into my office to wrap up and then left for home. I should have been mentally exhausted but I felt fired up. As if

I was super human and didn't need sleep. I'd been there before in the past when I'd come across a special deal. I wished that I was going to Maria's place but it wouldn't have been fair to wake her up.

I drive home through the quiet streets. The silence helped me relax and by the time I drove my car into the basement parking garage, the effects of the long day were creeping up on me. Our basement parking garage was so well lit that it resembled daylight. I got out of my car, locked it and took the elevator to my apartment.

I followed the same routine every night when I got home. I dropped my car keys on a table near the front door, kicked off my shoes and crossed the living room to the bedroom or kitchen, depending on whether I'd eaten dinner or not.

I dropped my keys, kicked off my shoes and was walking to the bedroom when I saw the figure of a stranger curled up on my couch, with a blanket draped over them. I went very still as my mind quickly tried to make sense of what I was seeing. What the fuck? Why would there be a woman sleeping on my couch?

Heart pounding crazily, I inched closer, taking care not to make any noise. When I got close enough to see her face, relief flooded me when I recognized Linda, Maria's sister. It still puzzled me what she was doing asleep in my apartment, but at least she wasn't a stranger. I backed off and made my way to the bedroom.

I wasn't as shocked to find Maria asleep on my bed. Not as I had been to see Linda. She had a key to my apartment and I was glad that she had made use of it. It would have been a thrill to find Maria in my bed but with Linda's presence, it worried me. I shrugged out of my jacket and went to the bathroom to wash my face and get ready to join Maria in bed.

The thought of her soft body molded against mine pushed away all the other thoughts. I finished in the bathroom and returned to the bedroom. Wearing only my boxer briefs, I slipped between the sheets and edged closer to Maria. She looked so peaceful and beautiful when she was asleep.

I smoothed back strands of her soft, silky hair and then bent down to kiss her forehead. Despite doing it softly and barely brushing my lips across her skin, she stirred and seconds later, her eyes fluttered open. She smiled and then to my shock, tears filled her eyes.

"You're finally home," she said.

"Why are you crying?" I said, concern growing inside me. It was not the normal so happy to see you tears. There was more to it and there was also the fact that Linda was asleep on my couch.

Instead of talking, Maria buried her face in my chest and cried, her body heaving. Fear clutched my heart. I tried to work out what had happened but nothing came to mind. "It's okay, I'm here now."

The story poured out of her. How she had wanted to surprise me and move in so that I'd find her home when I came from work. Her voice trembled when she got to the part where she had realized that she was bleeding. I held her tighter.

"Why didn't you call me?" I asked her.

"You're phone was switched off and I didn't want to bother you. I knew how important that meeting was," she said.

I cursed inwardly.

Her sisters had taken her to the ER and an ultrasound had established that the baby was okay. The heartbeat was strong and there was no cause to worry. What she needed was to take extra care of herself and not make the mistake of physically exerting herself.

"I was so scared Stephen," she said. "I thought we'd lost our baby."

I wanted to punch myself. I had put Maria in a position of thinking that she couldn't get hold of me and that my work was more important.

Your work comes first!

Paige's words scream in my head. I push them away. That's not true. My new family will come first. Then I recalled the excitement that had coursed through my blood when I'd been in that meeting. How I'd left no space for anything else but the deal we were thrashing out.

Had I been as caring as I was trying to portray, surely I'd have kept my phone switched on or at least turned it on several times to check if Maria had messaged or called me. Confusion filled my brain. I didn't know what to believe any more. All I knew was that I'd messed up and I hadn't been there for Maria when she'd desperately needed me to be.

～

The following morning when we woke up, Linda was gone but had left a humorous note saying she had enjoyed spending the night in a penthouse apartment. Maria and I laughed over it and moved to the kitchen to have breakfast.

"Your job is to relax and wait for your breakfast," I ordered her.

"You're not getting any arguments from me," she said. "The only thing I need to do is to touch base with the bakery." She slid onto the stool at the island and turned her attention to her phone.

Guilt grabbed me by the throat as I watched her. She deserved a better man than me. A man who didn't periodically bail out of his responsibilities at home, when an exciting business opportunity fell in front of him.

Rousing myself, I flung the fridge double doors open and took out the things we needed for breakfast. Scrambled eggs and pancakes. I lost myself in the cooking and soon, a tantalizing smell filled the kitchen. When breakfast was ready, I served it on the island and sat down next to Maria.

"Ryan is God sent," she said. "Everything is running smoothly and they don't need me to today."

"Please take a few days off. I know the doctor said that you're okay to go back to work but it wouldn't hurt to rest a bit," I said choosing my words carefully. It was a tricky balance, wanting to protect your child who was still in her mother's womb, without seeming like you were trying to control her.

After the fight we'd had after I hired Ryan without consulting Maria, I never wanted her to accuse me of trying to control her ever again.

"I was thinking of doing that," Maria said, surprising me.

I let out a breath I hadn't realized I'd been holding. "I'm glad. How are you feeling, any cramps or pains?"

She smiled. "That's the fifth time you've asked me since we woke up. I'm okay. I promise I'll let you know if I feel something that is out of the ordinary."

"Good," I said.

"So much for surprising you, huh?" she said and took a bite of her eggs.

"It was a surprise all right," I said, laughing softly at the memory of finding Linda asleep on the couch. "Did you know that Linda snored?"

Maria's eyes widened. "Really? What fun it's going to be to have something to tease her about. That explains why her boyfriends don't last. Ha!"

She asked me about the meeting and I gave her a rundown of how it had gone. After breakfast, I cleaned up and then we went to relax in the living room. I fished my laptop out of its case apologetically but I'd seen an email on my phone, from our legal department that needed my attention.

"I hope you don't mind if I do some work," I said. "It won't take me long."

"Not at all," Maria said. "Take as much time as you need. I have some subscription magazines I want to read." I got her iPad and gave it to her.

We relaxed on the couch, each of us engrossed in our work. When Maria read something interesting, she read a snippet out aloud for me. It was a nice easy morning, the only interruption being a call from Maria's mom.

Maria's face was wary as she spoke to her mother and her responses are one-word answers. It puzzled me and I made a mental note to ask her about it later. From what I had gathered, the Swans were a close family, unless something had happened between Maria and her mother that I was not aware of.

At the end of the conversation, she rattled off our address and then said bye.

"She wants to come over," Maria said. "I hope that it's okay."

"Why would you even ask that?" I demanded. "This is your home too, the same way it's mine. You can have anyone over that you want. Tell you what, I'll go to the office for a few hours and give you some space to visit with your mom. But first, I'll make you guys a light lunch. How does that sound?"

"You're as close to perfect as a man can get," Maria said, looking at me warmly.

A look that I didn't deserve. The first thing that I thought of when it became clear from Maria's conversation that her mother was coming over, was that I could pop into the office for an hour or so.

What kind of man was I? My fiancée had spotted the previous night and instead of learning my lesson, I was itching to get to my office. I really needed that deal to go smoothly. Word had gone round about the company and I'd gotten word that other investment companies had started sniffing around Delivery Magic.

The paperwork was not done yet and it made me nervous to think that anything could happen at this point. The deal could be stolen from right under our noses as long as both parties hadn't signed on the dotted line.

We needed to move fast, which meant documents needed to be read, scrutinized and then signed quickly. That was the nature of our work. Some deals took time but some needed to happen at super speed.

I was consumed and obsessed by work and it was leaving little room for anything else. Then I reminded myself that what Maria and I didn't have was a conventional relationship. She didn't have high expectations of me since our marriage was not based on romantic ideals. That made me feel a bit better.

I made a chicken salad for Maria and her mom and stored it in the fridge, after which I showered and got ready. Mrs. Swan came just when I was about to leave. We exchanged pleasantries and then I kissed Maria and left.

MARIA

"Why didn't you call me?" My mother asked as soon as Stephen left the apartment. "I had to hear about it from your sisters.

She followed me to the couch and sat at one end of it. "We used to be so close Maria. We talked about everything. Now you hardly ever call home or even visit but this…"

Her voice dripped with hurt. I couldn't get any words out. It felt as if sandpaper had been stuffed down my throat. We sat staring at each other. How did you tell the woman who brought you into the world, a woman you loved with all of your heart, that she had let you down?

"Tell me what I did wrong," she said, twisting her hands on her lap.

She couldn't be more nervous than I was. The intensity of emotion I'd had when talking about it with my sisters had faded, shrunk by the threat of losing my baby. I inhaled deeply. "Okay Mom, I'll tell you."

She inched closer.

"You picked Amber's happiness over mine," I said, glad that I was keeping my emotions under wraps, as Stephen would say.

My mother was visibly shocked but there was a flash of another emotion in her eyes. That gave me the courage to continue.

"You wanted me to give my baby to Amber and Jack. My baby." Tears finally filled my eyes as the memories of that day came over me. "How could you ask that of me, Mom?" I said, a sob choking me.

Then my mother is crying into her hands. "I'm sorry. I'm so sorry," she cries. She gets herself under control again and faces me. "I was wrong and I knew it as soon as the words were out of my mouth. I don't have an excuse Maria but I can tell you that Amber's happiness is not more important than yours. I'm sorry sweetheart."

She looks genuinely regretful over what happened and to be honest, my baby was still mine and Stephen's. No one could force you to do anything and even though she had suggested I give my baby to Amber, it hadn't been an order.

"Forgive me?" she said.

I took her hands into mine. "It's okay Mom. It's fine and yes, I forgive you. I was at fault too. I should not have agreed to it in the first place. I should've been honest like Linda."

It was a difficult conversation but I felt as if the wall between us had crumbled down. She asked about the spotting and I told her everything that had happened including moving in with Stephen. I braced myself for the recriminations but none came. She kept the same look of concern as I told her how I dragged my suitcases to the closet.

"I had a miscarriage once," she says softly when I was done speaking. "It still remains one of the most painful experiences of my life."

My heart squeezes for her. I'd come close but I couldn't forget the terror that had gripped me at the thought of losing my baby. "I'm sorry Mom."

"It was a long time ago."

We had lunch together in the kitchen and by the time she left, it felt as if we had broken the barrier that had been between us. Emotionally exhausted by the previous day, I took an afternoon nap and figured I'd be awake when Stephen came back home.

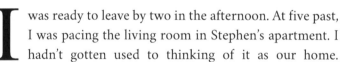

I was ready to leave by two in the afternoon. At five past, I was pacing the living room in Stephen's apartment. I hadn't gotten used to thinking of it as our home. Maybe after the wedding I would.

At ten past two, my phone vibrated with a message.

Stephen: I'm running late babe, can we meet at the venue?

Me: Sure. I'll see you there.

I swallowed my disappointment. My gaze bounced around the gorgeous house that had started to feel even bigger than it was. Work was stealing more and more of Stephen's time. In the last week, he hadn't gotten home earlier than eleven at night once.

I understood the excitement of the deal he was currently working on but never in my life had I ever witnessed someone driven by work as he was. I'd started to think that he had forgotten that I lived under the same roof and even about the baby.

Okay, suck it up. I took a deep, calming breath. It was probably my hormones that were making me so emotional. I resolutely ordered for an uber, grabbed my purse and left the apartment.

The uber was waiting downstairs and I slipped in and felt instantly cheered up to be making a move. With each passing minute I calmed down even more, knowing that I could handle whatever lay ahead.

The uber dropped me off at the venue and I waited outside the hotel for a few minutes before deciding that it was silly to wait for Stephen outside when I could be comfortable inside.

I found Mrs. Cohen and Marjorie, the wedding planner in the reception area. They both stood up when they saw me.

"Is Stephen joining us?" Marjorie asked.

I immediately jumped to his defense, surprising myself. "He's held up at work but he'll join us as soon as he can get away." I couldn't believe that those words had left my mouth.

I'd seen the same behavior from married couples, jumping to each other's defense. I'd always rolled my eyes when it happened but I started to understand. It came naturally. As though the other person's bad behavior was a reflection on you.

"Maria will update him on anything he misses," Mrs. Cohen said. "Let's begin."

Marjorie took us to the room in the hotel where the reception would be held. It was beautiful with two bars on each end. It was a huge room with ceiling to floor windows and French doors on one said with the view of the beautiful gardens. It was a venue I could imagine myself celebrating our reception.

"What do you think?" Marjorie asked, staring at me intently.

"It's beautiful," I said, my voice reverberating with the awe I felt. I didn't even want to think of how much it was going to cost.

The banquet manager joined us and we discussed menus. I loved the variety of the options they offered. I was impressed and afterwards, when we were standing outside the hotel about to say goodbye, I told Marjorie so.

"We have a few other places you can look at," she said with a happy smile. "But I have to tell you that this one tops them all."

I shook my head. The thought of looking at another venue without Stephen there to give his views was not attractive. "Let's go with this one. I love it and I'm sure Stephen will too."

"Great," Marjorie said.

She left and Mrs. Cohen and I were left alone.

"What happened with Stephen?" she said.

"He's in the middle of an investment that is taking a lot of his time," I said, feeling resentful all over again instead of the understanding fiancée that I wanted to be.

Mrs. Cohen chuckled. "His father was the same way. Sometimes he disappeared for weeks but I knew he was at the office and in the clutches of an awesome business idea."

She sounded proud of that particular trait of her late husband's.

"He would have starved if it hadn't been for the people who worked with him."

I shook my head. There was no way I was going to become like Mrs. Cohen. Overworking did not impress me. Balance in life was necessary and since we were going to have a child together, both of us needed to be there.

He doesn't love you!

The voice was as loud as if someone had spoken directly into my brain. If he didn't love me that meant that he couldn't or didn't want to make sacrifices for me. It hurt but it was the truth.

"Maria?"

I turned to Mrs. Cohen, startled. "Yes?"

"Are you okay?" she said. "You looked so far away for a minute there."

Heavy footsteps sounded and then Stephen was kissing me on the cheek. "I'm sorry babe. I lost track of time."

My heart twisted. If Stephen had loved me, if the marriage proposal had been based on honest genuine emotions, he wouldn't have lost track of time. That saddened me. Would a marriage of convenience be enough for me?

I wanted security for our baby, but I could provide that for her or him. The bakery had grown more than threefold since the conference that Stephen took me too. The revenue from our custom orders have surpassed our retail revenue. Stephen had been right. Custom orders were where the money was.

Stephen kissed his mother and then we all said goodbye and Stephen and I went to his car.

"You're very quiet?" he said. "Are you upset?"

"I'm fine," I said, my voice as weary as I felt.

"I'm sorry. You shouldn't have had to do that alone," he added.

I let my head fall back to the headrest, too tired to answer.

My sisters rallied around me the following week and came by the bakery whenever they were free. The wedding was getting closer and I was becoming a bundle of nerves.

"How are you feeling now that you're almost becoming Mrs. Cohen?" Amber asked me as we sat at the quiet bakery.

Everyone had left for the day and it was my turn to shut down for the day. Amber and Linda had fallen into our earlier pattern of having tea or coffee together in the evening before they left for home.

"You look tired," Linda said. "Be careful sis, we don't want a scare like we did the other time."

"It's not physical exhaustion," said. "The seriousness of getting married is hitting me harder. Plus, it's just dawned on me how much Stephen loves his job."

My sisters stared at me as though I'd lost my mind.

"Don't you love your job?" Linda said. "I love my job. I hope that if I ever do settle down, my partner will think of it as a positive thing."

"It is positive," I said, regretting that I'd said something about my recent feelings of ...I wasn't sure if it was neglect or worry that I was making a mistake. I couldn't pin it down.

"You're not making sense sis," Linda said.

"Let me try again. I love that Stephen loves his job but it's more than loving his job. For instance he's currently involved in this mega deal and he lives and breathes it. If I hadn't moved in with him, I'd rarely see him."

"Ah, you're feeling neglected." Amber said. "It happens but he'll come back to you when that deal is over."

"Take Saturday for example. We had a meeting with the wedding planner to see the venue. Stephen came when we had finished. He was at the office and had completely forgotten about it."

It had hurt deeply but that hadn't been the worst part.

"His mother told me that Stephen's dad had been the same way. He could go weeks neglecting his family when he was involved in something exciting. He lived for his business," I said.

"Stephen is not the same way surely?" Amber said.

"I think he might be," I said, voicing my real fears. Did I want to get married to someone who put everything else on hold while he went after a deal?

I hadn't even made my feelings known to Stephen either because our marriage was not going to be a real marriage. I had no proper claim on his time. I wasn't sure any more what I wanted.

"It's probably wedding jitters bringing all these fears to the surface," Amber said. "I was a mess just before our wedding. But they evaporated as soon as I saw Jack waiting for me at the front of the church."

That was the difference between Amber and Jack's relationship and mine and Stephen. Theirs was based on love.

"I have some news," Amber said.

Everything in me went still. Hope soared in my heart. Maybe it had finally happened for them. It would be so cool.

"No, it's not that," Amber continued. "I can see what you're thinking in both of your eyes."

I dropped my gaze and I was sure, Linda did the same.

"We're moving out of State. Jack got a transfer to a fire station in this seaside town in Florida."

"A beach town?" I squealed before if dawned on me that Amber and Jack moving meant that I was not going to have the kind of moments as we usually enjoyed, like coffee in the bakery after work.

"You're moving to another state?" Linda said.

Amber nodded. "I'll miss you guys too but look at the bright side. You'll have a vacation place any time you wish."

Linda and I were like a bunch of miserable wet blankets. Amber was clearly excited by the move but I couldn't bring myself to be happy for her. Things were changing too rapidly and I'd loved my life as it was.

I wanted both of my sisters in the same town as me. I wanted them to be there as Aunties for my child. The selfishness in that thought slammed into me and I saw how selfish I was being. Amber had been through a lot in the last few years, trying for a baby and getting disappointed every month.

Then there was this last fiasco for the surrogacy which had proven to be another crushing disappointment to her. Recalling all that made me understand why she was excited to go.

"Anyway, I have to go to Florida and look at some property that we want to buy. I'll also look at potential places for my business. You guys, this fills like a new beginning," she said.

"I would come with you but after taking time off for the wedding, I don't think I can wiggle more time off work," Linda said.

I thought fast. There was nothing keeping me here and I really needed some thinking time. Time to figure out what I wanted to do with my life. Peter, Ryan and Beth were running the bakery like a well-oiled machine. They could manage without me for a week.

"I'll come with you," I piped up. "I need a vacation."

MARIA

I knew why Stephen had taken me out for dinner. It was to placate me for the last couple of weeks but I was not in the mood to be placated. That was going to be the pattern of our lives if I allowed it. He would do as he pleased for as long as he wanted and then guilt would overwhelm him and he would shower me with attention before the cycle started again.

I was feeling good about myself having made the decision to go with Linda.

"When is our next appointment with the obstetrician?" Stephen asked me as he sat across from me eating, cutting up his steak.

"It was last week on Wednesday," I said.

He went still and stared at me. "You went alone?"

"Yeah, it's not a big deal. I've been doing everything else alone. The wedding arrangements, buying stuff for the baby." The resentment I'd been feeling for weeks bubbled up in my chest.

I acted nonchalant and continued eating my food while my heart pounded furiously. It was the first indication I'd ever given Stephen that I was not happy.

"Work has been crazy," he said, his voice faltering in a way I'd never heard him speak before.

I raised my head and met his gaze. His dark eyes gave nothing away.

"Amber and Jack are moving to Florida and I've offered to go with her and help her look at houses," I said coolly. "We're leaving tomorrow."

His eyes darkened. "You're going to Florida for a week?"

"Yes. Ryan and Peter have the bakery covered," I said.

"Is it safe to travel?" he finally said.

"Yes. Doctor White said that it's not a problem."

He was silent for a few seconds. "What about the wedding preparations? I'm sure there are a lot of loose ends to tie up this week."

I gave him a bright smile that I was sure did not reach my eyes. "I'm sure you can handle it. You don't need me for that."

I could see the hurt reflected in his eyes, but just like I couldn't ask him when he'd been spending all sorts of crazy hours at work, he couldn't ask the questions he would have liked to. Like how could I have made such a decision without discussing it with him?

It gave me a small measure of comfort to know that he was feeling how it felt to be on the other side. It didn't last. My heart went out to him but I wasn't going to back down. Stephen also needed to know what he was getting into and like me, he needed to make a decision on whether he really wanted that kind of marriage.

The atmosphere became chilly and for the rest of the dinner, we barely spoke. It was horrible. Everything in me ached. I sneaked a glance at Stephen and found his steady gaze on me.

Longing and aching came over me. I wanted more. Needed more. I wanted Stephen to whisper into my ear that he loved me. Our deal was not going to be enough for me. I'd broken it already. The truth slammed into me. I loved Stephen Cohen.

Feelings for him had snuck up on me. They had taken root and now, I loved him with all of my heart and soul. That would only lead to heartbreak. His rejection the last couple of weeks had hurt more than anything I'd ever experienced.

After dinner, Stephen paid the bill and we left and headed for home without exchanging a single word.

～

"This is so peaceful," Amber said as we strolled down the beach.

We'd arrived in the beach side resort late in the afternoon. Amber and I had decided to make it a semi vacation and have fun while we were at it. We'd made a schedule where we would be busy in the mornings looking at houses and business premises, then in the afternoon, we would hit the beach and relax.

So far from home, the seriousness of my problems hit me but at the same time, it gave me the distance I needed to make a decision about my future and that of my baby's.

My gaze fell on the gentle surface of the stark blue ocean. The scent of the salty air wafted up my nostrils refreshing my lungs. The beach was empty of people at that time of evening and Amber felt as if we were on a private beach.

"I can't believe you'll be living here," I said.

Amber chuckled. "I know. Who would have believed that I'd be excited to be leaving home?"

I reached for her hand and took it. "You've had a rough year."

"Yeah, I have. But like Jack said, it's time to focus on me and my business. I'm looking forward to that."

We walked silently for a few minutes before Amber spoke up. "How about you Sis? You're getting married in less than a week and yet you are here with me."

I inhaled sharply. "We agreed to get married for the sake of our baby. Stephen was adamant that he wanted the baby to be secure."

"There's nothing wrong with that," Amber said.

"On paper. In reality though, I don't know if I want to be in a marriage that is not founded on love."

I loved my baby and I wanted him or her to grow up with both parents in her life. But I didn't want to get married to a man I loved but who didn't love me back.

"But you two love each other!" Amber exclaimed.

"I love him but he doesn't love me," I admitted miserably. It was humiliating to admit that you loved someone and they didn't love you back.

"Bullshit!" Amber said. "I've seen how that man looks at you. Jack saw it too. He loves you even though he doesn't admit it."

I wished it was true. Amber and Jack were my family. They saw what they wanted to see.

"Don't tell me you want to call of the wedding," Amber said, coming to a stop.

"I don't know. This week will give me time to think and figure out what I want," I said.

We stood facing the sea, watching the sun slowly dip behind the clouds. I suddenly wished that I was watching the sunset with Stephen. I felt guilty at the thought. I hadn't been anywhere with any of my sisters in years. I promised myself to have fun and to banish Stephen from my thoughts.

"Time is a healer," Amber said. "In a way I'm glad that the surrogacy didn't work out but I'll never stop being grateful that you were willing to carry a baby for me."

"You're my sister. I'd do anything for you or Linda," I said.

We turned and started the walk back to the resort.

"I like the way your hand is always on your belly, as if soothing the baby," Amber said. "I hope that one day I'll get pregnant and experience having a baby growing in my belly."

"You will. It'll probably happen when you least expect it. When you're not stressing about it," I said.

"Jack says the same thing," Amber said. "I'm starting to believe it. I'm going days without thinking of babies."

"Did Jack ask for the transfer?" I said, voicing the question that had been nagging at me.

Amber didn't immediately answer which made me believe that my hunch was correct. It hurt to know that I was part of the reason why they were leaving, even though I understood it.

"Yes," Amber said and sighed. "He said it was either that or watch his wife losing her mind."

"It's tough been around me, huh?" I said. I'd been a fool thinking that the surrogacy business was behind us. It would always be a sore wound for Amber until she got her own baby.

"Sometimes but it's becoming better. That's why I was so happy when you offered to come with me. It's nice to spend time with you without dreaming that the baby you're carrying is mine and Jack's."

I took in a sharp breath. I'd been so busy planning a wedding and a fabulous life that I'd not given any thought to what Amber was going through.

"I'm a selfish bitch!" I said. "I'm so sorry I wasn't there for you Amber."

"There's nothing you could have done short of giving me your baby and clearly that wasn't an option," she said and grinned to show me that she was kidding.

"This is going to be a week of healing," I said.

"We'll drink to that tonight," Amber said.

We returned to our rooms in the resort and agreed to meet in an hour for dinner. I used that time to unpack and to have a quick shower. When I was done and had ten minutes to spare, I went to sit on the balcony that overlooked the beach.

My life seemed so uncertain when only months ago, I'd known what I wanted and where I was headed. Now I didn't even know if I was going to be married or not.

Everything seemed so complicated.

STEPHEN

"Thank God neither of us has expanded our waist lines," Jeremy said as we stood in the dressing room staring at our reflections in the mirror.

I grunted a response.

"What the fuck is wrong with you?" Jeremy exploded. "I've never seen you so moody?"

He clapped my back. "You're getting married man. You're supposed to be happy to have snagged the woman you want to spend the rest of your life with."

"It's impossible to be happy when you're not sure there's going to be a wedding," I said.

I had a feeling that Maria was not going to go through with the wedding and a part of me believed it was for the best.

Jeremy turned to face me. "What's going on man, I thought that you really wanted to do this?"

"I don't think I'm the kind of man she needs in her life," I said and proceeded to tell him about work and how it had consumed me.

"Did she complain about it?" Jeremy said.

"No, but I could see the hurt in her eyes," I said, feeling ashamed of myself as I made that admission.

"Why did you do it?" Jeremy said.

I shrugged. "I guess I wanted to see if we could take the heat, as a couple. See if we would make it when we were married."

Jeremey narrowed his eyes. "You don't test the people you love Stephen."

I opened my mouth to protest the love part. I sucked in a breath as the truth I'd been running away confronted me. I loved Maria. I'd loved her from the moment I clapped my eyes on her.

For me, it had been love at first sight and since then, I'd done everything in my power to subtly sabotage what we had. I'd pushed her away and the knowledge made my chest ache with a deep pain.

"I'm no therapist, but it sounds to me as if you're afraid of your own feelings," Jeremy said.

I fiddled with my collar and ignored Jeremy but my mind was busy sifting through my emotions. Was it true that I was afraid of my own feelings? Was I afraid of being a husband and a dad?

After Paige and I divorced, I'd vowed to never get married again but that had changed when Maria got pregnant. At first, I'd hidden behind the baby, saying that I wanted to do right by our baby. But even then, I'd loved her but I'd not been ready to admit it to myself.

I didn't want to go into marriage with Maria while hiding behind words like obligation and responsibility. I wanted to open my heart to her and marry her with the full knowledge that I loved her. I wanted to believe that she loved me too. I couldn't bear to contemplate the possibility that she didn't love me.

"Are we done here?" I said and shrugged out of the tuxedo jacket. "I have to go and convince my fiancée to marry me."

I texted Amber before I got on the flight and asked her for the name of where they were staying. I also asked her to keep it to herself as I wanted to surprise Maria. It wasn't so much that I wanted to surprise her but that I didn't want to give her time to think of reasons why she was not going to marry me.

I had a feeling that her plan was to call off the wedding and I needed every ammunition available to me. I'd been a complete asshole to her. On the flight to Florida, I recalled the pain in her eyes when she had told me about going to the doctor alone.

Even now, thinking about it, made me feel as if someone was twisting a sword in my heart. How could I have allowed my fears to come between what I wanted most in my life?

I couldn't use my father's inability to be a good father as a reason not to give it my all. It was a decision that one made to either be a good parent or not to be. To be available for your family or to let your work come first and your family last.

I loved my work but I wanted more, not that I'd tasted life with love in it. Maria had splashed color and joy into my life. My home had become a happy place rather than somewhere I went to lay down to rest.

I couldn't wait until our home was filled with the sounds of a crying baby. The things that new parents complained about were the things I was looking forward to. Pacing at night with our baby cradled in my arms and soothing them to sleep. Having my sleep interrupted by a little human.

I was looking forward to that, which was a shocker, considering that I loved an organized life. Now I craved chaos in my life. Chaos caused by love. But first, I needed to convince Maria that she was not making a mistake in marrying me.

I took a cab from the airport and when I got to the resort, I checked in, dumped my bag in the room and headed to the beach. I strolled along the beach, trying not to be creepy and stare at people in the search for my fiancée.

I saw her laying on a beach lounger and Amber beside her, craning her neck in my direction. When she saw me, she sat up and waited.

I shot Amber a smile and sunk to my knees beside Maria's lounger. Sensing someone beside her, she cracked one eye open and when she saw me, she let out a shriek and sat up.

"Hey," I said.

"Hi," Maria said. "How did you know where we were?"

"I have my sources," I said playfully.

A guarded look came over her features. I ignored the pain that shot through me. I deserved it. I was the one who had put that look of wariness on her face. She had stopped trusting me to make her happy.

I glanced up for a second at the gorgeous sunset. Splashes of orange and gold and purple. It was the perfect background to propose marriage to the woman you loved, knowing that she loved you back and wanted to spend the rest of her life with you.

I was not in that lucky position and nervousness almost got the better of me. I'd never walked into a conference room or anywhere else for that matter without the uttermost confidence that I was going to win. I'd never been in the position I was in where the odds were stacked against me.

I cleared my throat. I'd practiced on the airplane but suddenly my mind was empty, except for one sentence.

I took her hand into mine. "Maria Swan, will you marry me?"

Her eyes narrowed as she stared at me quizzically. "But I already agreed to marry you Stephen," she said.

"Yes, you did but this time the stakes are higher. I'm asking you to love me, Maria. To marry me for love, not for convenience."

She continued staring at me.

"I've loved you from the moment I first saw you in your bakery. You touched a part of me that had remain untouched all my life. The more I got to know you, the more I fell in love with you. The avalanche of feelings I had for you frightened me, Maria. That's the only reason I behaved like a complete asshole."

Her lips curved into a tiny smile. It gave me the courage to continue.

"I'm so sorry babe, I don't deserve you or our baby but somehow, I've struck gold and you are in my life."

"What happens the next time a sweet deal falls into your lap? Do we stop existing for weeks?" she said, hurt in her voice.

"It won't happen again and if it does, which it won't, you're to march into my office and demand that I go home."

She laughed.

I cupped her face. "I love you Maria. Please say you'll marry me and love me."

Her features softened. "I love you, Stephen. That's the only reason I'm going to say yes."

"That's the only reason I need," I said and leaned forward to kiss her. It was meant to be a light kiss but as soon as our mouths touched, raw, wild need passed between us.

Our breaths came out ragged as the kiss deepened. My whole body shook with relief, emotion and a need to possess her. The little common sense that remained restrained me, reminding me that we were on a public beach.

"I want to show you my room," Maria said, pursing her lips suggestively.

I managed a laugh that came out like a hack. "Let's go."

"Amber disappeared," Maria said with a laugh. "I guess we bordered on X-rated."

I held her hand and we returned to the resort. I couldn't believe that she wanted me in her life. That she loved me. If I hadn't learned to keep my emotions in check since I was a young kid, I'd have cried.

In her room, we shut the door and I pulled her to me with a growl. I raked my fingers through her hair. "I've missed you so much Maria. I was so frightened that I'd lost you."

"Me too," she said, tears filling her eyes.

I used my thumb to outline her lips and then I brought my mouth to hers, intending to kiss her gently but ended up crashing her lips with mine. I slid my hands under her t-shirt and cupped her breasts over her bikini top.

Maria moaned into my mouth flaming my desire. I pressed her against my swollen dick wanting her to feel my need for her.

"It's been so long," I said, pulling back to undress her. "I've missed this hot body."

"I've missed you too," Maria said, palming my chest before she turned her attention to the buttons of my shirt. Impatiently, she pushed the shirt over my head and I helped her the rest of the way.

I lifted her top over her head and stood still for a moment to admire the swell of her breasts and the gentle curve of her belly. "You're so fucking gorgeous Maria."

I took my time removing her bra followed by her shorts and panties. Then she was standing gloriously, sexily in front of me, looking too beautiful to touch.

"Are you just going to stand there devouring me with your eyes?" Maria asked playfully.

I stepped forward and pressed her to me. Heat enveloped me and it took every ounce of control not to lay her on the bed and take her savagely. I kissed her as gently as I could, exploring her mouth with my tongue as if it was the first time.

"I want you Stephen," Maria said.

I cupped her breasts and lowered my head to take a nipple into my mouth. She gripped my head and moaned loudly. As I teased her nipples, I snaked a hand between her legs and stroked her wet folds.

She felt so fucking good. So hot and so ready for me. She pushed me gently from her breasts, and lay down on the bed. "There'll be time for games later," she said in husky voice. "Now, I want you inside me."

I was sure that I'd ripped my pants when I pulled them down along with my boxers. I stepped out of them and joined Maria on the bed. I arranged my body lengthwise against hers and kissed her deeply again.

"Please Stephen, I need you," she said, nudging me on top of her.

"You've got me." I spread her thighs open and inhaled sharply when I caught a glimpse of her gleaming folds. "Enough talk." It was time to worship my soon to be wife, with my hands, mouth, tongue and everything in me.

MARIA

"You are amazingly calm for someone who spent the last week before her wedding in Florida instead of seeing to last minute duties," Linda said as she zipped me up.

The bridal store had done a good job estimating the growth of my pregnant belly and the dress fitted me perfectly. I couldn't believe that it was the morning of my wedding. All of us girls had spent the night at the hotel and had reserved a suite to get ready for the wedding.

We had spent half the night reminiscing about the past especially our growing up years. Going back in time had made me appreciate what a happy childhood I'd had. I wanted the same for our baby and the family we would get later.

Stephen had gone for a drink with his best friend Jeremy and Amber's husband Jack. I was glad that the two men who would soon be brothers-in-law had taken to each other.

"How does it feel to be getting married to someone you love?" Linda asked me as she fussed with my veil.

Tears sprouted into my eyes but I blamed that on my hormones. I was in the second trimester and I'd heard that it was an emotional time for the mother as that was the period when the baby experienced very fast growth.

"It's unbelievable," I said. "I expected wedding jitters but all I feel is a sense of peace and anticipation, I guess. I can't wait to see Stephen in his tuxedo. I bet he'll look amazing."

"He could be in an old pair of swimming trunks and you'd think he looked amazing," Amber said, having caught my last sentence.

We had already had our hair and makeup done and my sisters helping me to dress was the last thing to do before we had to make our way to the garden where the formal ceremony was being held.

"You look beautiful," Linda said, standing in front of me to stare at my face through the veil. "Come and look at yourself." She took my hand and led me to the mirror.

I peered at my reflection. I did look pretty. I couldn't believe that I was actually going to get married and to a man whom I loved with all of my heart. I couldn't imagine saying I do to anyone else apart from Stephen.

"Thank you," I said.

Amber came to stand on my other side. "You're the most beautiful bride in the whole world little sister."

I lay my head on her shoulder. "Thank you. I hope Stephen thinks the same thing too."

A knock came on the door and before either of us could move, it swung open and my mother entered the room.

"Would you look at you?" she said, staring at me. "You're glowing Maria."

She came to me and took my hands. "I am so proud of you. You chose well. Stephen is a wonderful man and he loves you so much."

"I love him too Mom," I said, remembering the stories that had been in the tabloids once word got out that Stephen Cohen was getting married.

Luckily, they hadn't gone crazy with it but the few stories that had appeared had implied that I'd trapped Stephen with marriage. Somehow, they had found out that I was pregnant.

"We're the ones who matter," Stephen had said so many times until I'd stopped stressing over the accusation.

My mom and I hugged and when she left, things started happening fast.

"See you guys in a bit," Linda said and kissed my cheek.

Amber glanced at her watch. "It's almost time. I love how serene you look."

I grinned. "I feel happy."

"Good, that's how every bride should feel on her wedding day," Amber said. "Stephen will be blown away when he sees you. He'll hoist you on his shoulder and take you to a room," she added with a giggle.

I laughed too at the images her words formed. "That's the plan."

My dad was waiting for us downstairs and when he saw me, he opened his arms and I walked right into them.

"I'm so proud of you," he whispered into my ear.

We made our way to the French doors that led to the garden where the wedding ceremony was being held. Marjorie was waiting near the doors and when she saw me, she took a few minutes to rearrange my veil.

"See you later," Amber said, blowing me a kiss.

The wedding march came on and it was time for my father and me to walk down the aisle. All sorts of feelings came over me as we made our way down the makeshift, beautifully decorated aisle.

I waved at friends and family and then as I got nearer, I caught and held Stephen's gaze. He looked at me as if I was his most prized possession. I was sure I held the same expression in my eyes. After that I had no eyes for anyone else except my husband to me.

The formal ceremony went by too fast and Stephen surprised me by adding his own words to the vows. Then we were husband and wife and he was holding me tightly in his arms and kissing me as if there was no one else witnessing the intimate moment.

I smiled like an idiot as we got our pictures taken in the beautifully landscaped gardens and as we went to the ballroom where the reception was being held.

Jeremy gave a funny touching speech, giving anecdotes of the years they grew up together and how he never thought that Stephen would meet a woman who made him turn into a blabbering idiot.

Then it was time for us to dance, the moment I'd been waiting for all day. Stephen enclosed me in his arms and I rested my head on his chest.

"God, I love you so much, do you know that?" He murmured.

"I do. I really do."

"This is the part where you're supposed to say you love me back," he said with a chuckle.

"You know I do," I said. "I love you so much. I didn't ever think it was possible to feel as happy as I do."

EPILOGUE

MARIA

"This baby is refusing to bulge," I complained to Stephen as we sat in the living room with my feet on his lap. "I'm tired of being pregnant."

I made a face. "I'm sorry for complaining," I said. The baby's due date had come and passed and still he was making no move to leave the oven.

"He'll come when he's ready," Stephen said serenely. "And you have every right to complain. It can't be easy carrying our firecracker when he's become so big."

"I love you," I said with a tired smile. "You're a saint for putting up with me."

"You've been wonderful," Stephen said.

I'd stuffed myself with dates and anything else I heard helped get those labor pains going. Then he kicked me but it wasn't like the regular dull kicks. This one was actually painful.

"Ouch," I said and made a face. "Why would you kick your mother so painfully?"

Stephen rubbed my belly. The next thing I felt was a cramp which seemed to spread to my whole body.

"I think this is it," I said to Stephen.

Stephen's eyes widened and then he jumped to his feet and started pacing. I was frightened but seeing him like that made me burst into laughter. "What are you doing?" I said.

He looked at me as if what he was doing was obvious. "Thinking. I can't remember what we were told at the childbirth education classes."

It was fascinating to watch him. Stephen always kept his cool, no matter what and seeing him lose it was like watching a movie. Another sharp pain came and I stopped watching Stephen.

"Let's call the doctor," he said.

"No, not yet. It's too early. Remember what the doctor said. We need to time ourselves first."

We moved to the bedroom where it was more comfortable. Stephen had regained his composure and he continued massaging my back and feet. Somewhere close to midnight, the cramps changed and I knew that I was in active labor.

As we made our way to the car, my water broke and my panic set in. What if I gave birth on the way to the hospital?

"Remember what the doctor said," Stephen said as he settled me in the car. "The first baby takes time to get out."

"I don't think there's going to be another one Stephen," I said just before a painful contraction.

"Whatever you say my queen," he said.

There was no traffic at that time of night and we made it to the hospital in under ten minutes. I was wheeled into triage and then taken to my room.

"I love you so much," Stephen said, smoothing my hair back.

"I love you too," I said.

It had been an incredible five months that we'd lived together. Stephen had kept his promise and had refused to let work consume him. He picked me up from the bakery every evening even though I could drive myself.

Those five months had been the happiest of my life. The bakery was doing well too and we'd even won the award for the fastest growing bakery in the state. My sisters were doing well too. Linda was still engrossed in her job but I suspected that she was secretly seeing someone.

She had a glow that hadn't been there months back. Amber was happy and busy in Florida with her new home and business. She was waiting for word that her nephew had been born and then she and Jack would come visit.

"Another one is coming," Stephen said, jolting me back to the present.

The nurse had shown him how to read the monitor to tell when a contraction was about to come. I braced myself and as the searing pain came, it felt as though my body was being ripped in two.

At some point, Dr. White came in but by that point, I was incoherent with pain. Stephen kept my hand in his, the whole time even though I was sure that I'd come close to breaking his wrist several times.

At 5.45AM, Aiden Cohen, made his way into the world, his tiny eyes as dark as his dad's and wide open, not wanting to miss any part of the world.

Later, after we'd both been cleaned up and he'd latched on successfully, Stephen and I shared a few minutes alone with our baby before our family descended on us.

I cradled him while Stephen stared at us both in wonder.

"We're a family of three now," he said. "I can't wait to take Aiden home."

"Me too," I said, starring down at my son who would always remind me of his dad. "He looks so much like you."

Stephen chuckled. "You'll have to work a lot harder next time if you want your genes passed on."

I laughed. "And how do I do that?"

"Be creative," Stephen said and we both laughed.

The door burst open and Stephen's mom, closely followed by my mom, dad and Linda entered the room, exclaiming over the baby. Stephen moved away from the bed saying he risked being trampled on.

"He's so handsome," my mother cooed.

"And a happy disposition," Stephen's mom said. "Just like Stephen had been as a baby."

Stephen and I exchanged a look from across the room. We had made it, as unlikely as it had seemed at the beginning. Love had sprouted from a marriage of convenience and had grown to unimaginable proportions. I couldn't imagine my life without him and now without our Baby Aiden.

The End.

ABOUT THE AUTHOR

Thank you so much for reading!
If you have enjoyed the book and would like to leave a
precious review for me, please kindly do so here:

Charming The Enemy

Please click on the link below to receive info about my latest
releases and giveaways.
NEVER MISS A THING

Or
come and say hello here:

Made in United States
Orlando, FL
06 June 2022

18533892R00186